Tales of New England

BY

SARAH ORNE JEWETT.

HOUGHTON, MIFFLIN & CO.

TALES OF NEW ENGLAND

BY

SARAH ORNE JEWETT

BOSTON AND NEW YORK
HOUGHTON, MIFFLIN AND COMPANY
The Riverside Press, Cambridge
1895

CONTENTS.

———·———

Sarah Orne Jewett (September 3, 1849 – June 24, 1909) was an American novelist, short story writer and poet, best known for her local color works set along or near the southern seacoast of Maine. Jewett is recognized as an important practitioner of American literary regionalism.

Jewett's family had been residents of New England for many generations, and Sarah Orne Jewett was born in South Berwick, Maine.Her father was a doctor specializing in "obstetrics and diseases of women and children." and Jewett often accompanied him on his rounds, becoming acquainted with the sights and sounds of her native land and its people.As treatment for rheumatoid arthritis, a condition that developed in early childhood, Jewett was sent on frequent walks and through them also developed a love of nature. In later life, Jewett often visited Boston, where she was acquainted with many of the most influential literary figures of her day; but she always returned to South Berwick, small seaports near which were the inspiration for the towns of "Deephaven" and "Dunnet Landing" in her stories.

Jewett was educated at Miss Olive Rayne's school and then at Berwick Academy, graduating in 1866. She supplemented her education through an extensive family library. Jewett was "never overtly religious," but after she joined the Episcopal church in 1871, she explored less conventional religious ideas. For example, her friendship with Harvard law professor Theophilus Parsons stimulated an interest in the teachings of Emanuel Swedenborg, an eighteenth-century Swedish scientist and theologian, who believed that the Divine "was present in innumerable, joined forms — a concept underlying Jewett's belief in individual responsibility."

She published her first important story in the Atlantic Monthly at age 19, and her reputation grew throughout the 1870s and 1880s. Her literary importance arises from her careful, if subdued, vignettes of country life that reflect a contemporary interest in local color rather than plot. Jewett possessed a keen descriptive gift that William Dean Howells called "an uncommon feeling for talk — I hear your people." Jewett made her reputation with the novella The Country of the Pointed Firs (1896).A Country Doctor (1884), a novel reflecting her father and her early ambitions for a medical career, and A White Heron (1886), a collection of short stories are among her finest work. Some of Jewett's poetry was collected in Verses (1916), and she also wrote three children's books. Willa Cather described Jewett as a significant influence on her development as a writer, and "feminist critics have since championed her writing for its rich account of women's lives and voices."

MISS TEMPY'S WATCHEES.

THE time of year was April; the place was a small farming town in New Hampshire, remote from any railroad. One by one the lights had been blown out in the scattered houses near Miss Tempy Dent's ; but as her neighbors took a last look out-of-doors, their eyes turned with instinctive curiosity toward the old house, where a lamp burned steadily. They gave a little sigh. " Poor Miss Tempy!" said more than one bereft acquaintance ; for the good woman lay dead in her north chamber, and the light was a watcher's light. The funeral was set for the next day, at one o'clock.

The watchers were two of the oldest friends, Mrs. Crowe and Sarah Ann Binson. They were sitting in the kitchen, because it seemed less awesome than the unused best room, and they beguiled the long hours by steady conversation. One would think that

neither topics nor opinions would hold out, at that rate, all through the long spring night; but there was a certain degree of ex-citernent just then, and the two women hud risen to an unusual level of expressivt n< ss and confidence. Each had already told the other more than one fact that she had determined to keep secret; they were again and again tempted into statements that either would have found impossible by daylight. Mrs. Crowe was knitting a blue yarn stocking for her husband; the foot was already so long that it seemed as if she must have forgotten to narrow it at the proper time. Mrs. Crowe knew exactly what she was about, however; she was of a much cooler disposition than Sister Binson, who made futile attempts at some sewing, only to drop her work into her lap whenever the talk was most engaging.

Their faces were interesting, — of the dry, shrewd, quick-witted New England type, with thin hair twisted neatly back out of the way. Mrs. Crowe could look vague and benignant, and Miss Binson was, to quote her neighbors, a little too sharp-set; but the world knew that she had need to be, with the load she must carry of supporting an ineffi-

cient widowed sister and six unpromising and unwilling nieces and nephews. The eldest boy was at last placed with a good man to learn the mason's trade. Sarah Ann Bin-son, for all her sharp, anxious aspect, never defended herself, when her sister whined and fretted. She was told every week of her life that the poor children never would have had to lift a finger if their father had lived, and yet she had kept her steadfast way with the little farm, and patiently taught the young people many useful things, for which, as everybody said, they would live to thank her. However pleasureless her life appeared to outward view, it was brimful of pleasure to herself.

Mrs. Crowe, on the contrary, was well to do, her husband being a rich farmer and an easy-going man. She was a stingy woman, but for all that she looked kindly; and when she gave away anything, or lifted a finger to help anybody, it was thought a great piece of beneficence, and a compliment, indeed, which the recipient accepted with twice as much gratitude as double the gift that came from a poorer and more generous acquaintance. Everybody liked to be on good terms with Mrs. Crowe. Socially she stood much

higher than Sarah Ann Binson. They were both old schoolmates and friends of Temperance Dent, who had asked them, one day, not long before she died, if they would not come together and look after the house, and manage everything, when she was gone. JBhe may have had some hope that they might become closer friends in this period of intimate partnership, and that the richer woman might better understand the burdens of the poorer. They had not kept the house the night before; they were too weary with the care of their old friend, whom they had not left until all was over.

There was a brook which ran down the hillside very near the house, and the sound of it was much louder than usual. When there was silence in the kitchen, the busy stream had a strange insistence in its wild voice, as if it tried to make the watchers understand something that related to the past.

" I declare, I can't begin to sorrow for Tempy yet. I am so glad to have her at rest," whispered Mrs. Crowe. " It is strange to set here without her, but I can't make it clear that she has gone. I feel as if she had got easy and dropped off to sleep, and I 'in more scared about waking her up than knowing any other feeling."

"Yes," said Sarah Ann, "it's just like that, ain't it ? But I tell you we are goin' to miss her worse than we expect. She 's helped me through with many a trial, has Temperance. I ain't the only one who says the same, neither."

These words were spoken as if there were a third person listening; somebody beside Mrs. Crowe. The watchers could not rid their minds of the feeling that they were being watched themselves. The spring wind whistled in the window crack, now and then, and buffeted the little house in a gusty way that had a sort of companionable effect. Yet, on the whole, it was a very still night, and the watchers spoke in a half-whisper.

" She was the freest-handed woman that ever I knew," said Mrs. Crowe, decidedly. " According to her means, she gave away more than anybody. I used to tell her 't wa'n't right. I used really to be afraid that she went without too much, for we have a duty to ourselves."

Sister Binson looked up in a half-amused, unconscious way, and then recollected herself.

Mrs. Crowe met her look with a serious face. " It ain't so easy for me to give as it

is for some," she said simply, but with an effort which was made possible only by the occasion. " I should like; to say, while Tempy xis laying here yet in her own house, that she has been a constant lesson to me. Folks are too kind, and shame me with thanks for what I do. I ain't such a generous woman as poor Tempy was, for all she had nothin' to do with, as one may say."

Sarah Binson was much moved at this confession, and was even pained and touched by the unexpected humility. " You have a good many calls on you " — she began, and then left her kind little compliment half finished.

" Yes, yes, but I 've got means enough. My disposition 's more of a cross to me as I grow older, and I made up my mind this morning that Tempy's exain shojdd be my pattern henceforth." She began to knit faster than ever.

" 'T ain 't no use to get morbid : that's what Tempy used to say herself," said Sarah Ann, after a minute's silence. " Ain't it strange to say ' used to say ' ? " and her own voice choked a little. " She never did like to hear folks git goin' about themselves."

" 'T was only because they 're apt to do it

so as other folks will say 't was n't so, an' praise 'em up," humbly replied Mrs. Crowe, " and that ain't my object. There wa'n't a child but what Tempy set herself to work to see what she could do to please it. One time my brother's folks had been stopping here in the summer, from Massachusetts. The children was all little, and they broke up a sight of toys, and left 'em when they were going away. Tempy come right up after they rode by, to see if she couldn't help me set the house to rights, and she caught me just as I was going to fling some of the clutter into the stove. I was kind of tired out, starting 'em off in season. ' Oh, give me them ! ' says she, real pleading; and she wropped 'em up and took 'em home with her when she went, and she mended 'em up and stuck 'em together, and made some young one or other happy with every blessed one. You'd thought I'd done her the biggest favor. ' No thanks to me. I should ha' burnt 'em, Tempy,' says I."

" Some of 'em came to our house, I know," said Miss Binson. " She 'd take a lot o' trouble to please a child, 'stead o' shoving of it out o' the way, like the rest of us when we 're drove."

" I can tell you the biggest thing she ever done, and I don't know's there's :myl>o<ly left but me to tell it. I don't want it forgot," Sarah Binson went on, looking up at the clock to see how the night was going. " It was that pretty-looking Trevor girl, who taught the Corners school, and married so well afterwards, out in New York State. You remember her, I dare say ? "

" Certain," said Mrs. Crowe, with an air of interest.

" She was a splendid scholar, folks said, and give the school a great start; but she 'd overdone herself getting her education, and working to pay for it, and she all broke down one spring, and Tetnpy made her come and stop with her a while, — you remember that ? Well, she had an uncle, her mother's brother, out in Chicago, who was well off and friendly, and used to write to Lizzie Trevor, and I dare say make her some presents ; but he was a lively, driving man, and did n't take time to stop and think about his folks. He had n't seen her since she was a little girl. Poor Lizzie was so pale and weakly that she just got through the term o' school. She looked as if slu> was just going straight off in a decline. Tenipy, she

cosseted her up a while, and then, next thing folks knew, she was tellin' round how Miss Trevor had gone to see her uncle, and meant to visit Niagary Falls on the way, and stop over night. Now I happened to know, in ways I won't dwell on to explain, that the poor girl was in debt for her schoolin' when she come here, and her last quarter's pay had just squared it off at last, and left her without a cent ahead, hardly ; but it had fretted her thinking of it, so she paid it all; those might have dunned her that she owed it to. An' I taxed Tempy about the girl's goin' off on such a journey till she owned up, rather 'n have Lizzie blamed, that she 'd given her sixty dollars, same 's if she was rolling in riches, and sent her off to have a good rest and vacation."

" Sixty dollars! " exclaimed Mrs. Crowe. "Tempy only had ninety dollars a year that came in to her; rest of her livin' she got by helpin' about, with what she raised off this little piece o' ground, sand one side an' clay the other. An' how often I 've heard her tell, years ago, that she 'd rather see Niagary than any other sight in the world ! "

The women looked at each other in silence; the^magpitude of the generous sacri-
fice was almost too great for their comprehension.

" She was just poor enough to do that! " declared Mrs. Crowe at last, in an abandon ment of feeling. " Say what you may, I feel humbled to the dust," and her coin]Kin-ion ventured to say nothing. She never had given away sixty dollars at once, but it was simply because she never had it to give. It came to her very lips to say in explanation. "Tempy was so situated;" but she clu-ckcd herself in time, for she would not betray her own loyal guarding of a dependent household.

"Folks say a great deal of generosity, and this one's being public-sperited, and that one free-handed about giving," said Mrs. Crowe, who was a little nervous in the silence. " I suppose we can't tell the sorrow it would be to some folks not to give, same's 'twould be to me not to save. I seem kind of made for that, as if 't was what I'd got to do. I should feel sighfs In-ttcr about it if I could make it evident what I was savin' for. If I had a child, now, Sarah Ann," and her voice was a little husky. — "if I had a child, I should think 1 was heapin' of it up because lie was the one

trained by the Lord to scatter it again for good. But here 's Mr. Crowe and me, we can't do anything with money, and both of us like to keep things same 's they Ve always been. Now Priscilla Dance was talking away like a mill-clapper, week before last. She 'd think I would go right off and get one o* them new-fashioned gilt-and-white papers for the best room, and some new furniture, an' a marble-top table. And I looked at her, all struck up. ' Why,' says I, ' Priscilla, that nice old velvet paper ain't hurt a mite. I should n't feel 't was my best room without it. Dan'el says 't is the first thing he can remember rubbin' his little baby fingers on to it, and how splendid he thought them red roses was.' I maintain," continued Mrs. Crowe stoutly, "that folks wastes sights o' good money cloin' just such foolish things. Tearin' out the iusides o' meetin'-houses, and fixin' the pews different; 't was good enough as 't was with mendin'; then times come, an' they want to put it all back same 's 't was before."

This touched upon an exciting subject to active members of that parish. Miss Bin-son and Mrs. Crowe belonged to opposite parties, and had at one time come as near hard

feelings as they could, and yet escape them. Each hastened to speak of other things and to show her untouched friendlin

" I do agree with you," said Sister Binson, " that few of us know what use to make of money, heyond every-day necessities. You 've seen more o' the world than I have, and know what's expected. When it comes to taste and judgment about such things, I ought to defer to others; " and with this modest avowal the critical moment passed when there might have been an improper discussion.

In the silence that followed, the fact of their presence in a house of death grew more clear than before. There was something disturbing in the noise of a mouse gnawing at the dry boards of a closet wall near by. Both the watchers looked up anxiously at the clock; it was almost the middle of the night, and the whole world seemed to have left them alone with their solemn duty. Only the brook was awake.

"Perhaps we might give a look up-stairs now," whispered Mrs. Crowe, as if she hoped to hear some reason against their going just then to the chamber of death : but Sister Binson rose, with a serious and yet

satisfied countenance, and lifted the small lamp from the table. She was much more used to watching than Mrs. Crowe, and much less affected by it. They opened the door into a small entry with a steep stairway ; they climbed the creaking stairs, and entered the cold upper room on tiptoe. Mrs. Crowe's heart began to beat very fast as the kmp was put on a high bureau, and made long, fixed shadows about the walls. She went hesitatingly toward the solemn shape under its white drapery, and felt a sense of remonstrance as Sarah Ann gently, but in a business-like way, turned back the thin sheet.

" Seems to me she looks pleasanter and pleasanter," whispered Sarah Ann Binson impulsively, as they gazed at the white face with its wonderful smile. "To-morrow 't will all have faded out. I do believe they kind of wake up a day or two after they die, and it '3 then they go." She replaced the light covering, and they both turned quickly away ; there was a chill in this upper room.

" 'T is a great thing for anybody to have got through, ain't it?" said Mrs. Crowe softly, as she began to go down the stairs on tiptoe. The warm air from the kitchen

beneath met them with a sense of welcome and shelter.

" I don' know why it is, but I feel as near again to Tempy down here as I do up there," replied Sister Binson. " I feel as if the air was full of her, kind of. I can sense things, now and then, that she seems to say. Now I never was one to take up with no nonsense of sperits and such, but I declare I felt as if she told me just now to put some more wood into the stove."

Mrs. Crowe preserved a gloomy silence. She had suspected before this that her companion was of a weaker and more credulous disposition than herself. " 'T is a great thing to have got through," she repeated, ignoring definitely all that had last been said. " I suppose you know as well as I that Tempy was one that always feared death. Well, it's all put behind her now ; she knows what ' t is." Mrs. Crowe gave a little sigh, and Sister Binson's quick sympathies were stirred toward this other old friend, who also dreaded the great change.

" I 'd never like to forgit almost those last words Tempy spoke plain to me," she said gently, like the comforter she truly w:is. " She looked up at me once or twice, that

last afternoon after I come to set by her, and let Mis' Owen go home ; and I says, 4 Can I do anything to ease you, Tempy ?' and the tears come into my eyes so I could n't see what kind of a nod she give me. ' No, Sarah Ann, you can't, dear,' says she ; and then she got her breath again, and says she, looking at me real meanin', ' I 'm only a-gettin' sleepier and sleepier; that's all there is,' says she, and smiled up at me kind of wishful, and shut her eyes. I knew well enough all she meant. She 'd been lookin' out for a chance to tell me, and I don' know's she ever said much afterwards."

Mrs. Crowe was not knitting; she had been listening too eagerly. " Yes, 't will be a comfort to think of that sometimes," she said, in acknowledgment.

" I know that old Dr. Prince said once, in evenin' meetin', that he 'd watched by many a dyin' bed, as we well knew, and enough o' his sick folks had been scared o' dyin' their whole lives through; but when they come to the last, he 'd never seen one but was willin', and most were glad, to go. ' 'T is as natural as bein' born or livin' on,' he said. I don't know what had moved him to speak that night. You know he wa'n't

TEMPTS WATCHERS.

in the habit of it, and 't was the monthly concert of prayer for foreign missions anyways," said Sarah Ann ; " but't was a great stay to the mind to listen to his words of experience."

" There never was a better man," responded Mrs. Crowe, in a really cheerful tone. She had recovered from her feeling of nervous dread, the kitchen was so comfortable with lamplight and firelight; and just then the old clock began to tell the hour of twelve with leisurely whirring strokes.

Sister Binson laid aside her work, and rose quickly and went to the cupboard. " We 'd better take a little to eat," she explained. " The night will go fast after this. I want to know if you went and made some o' your nice cupcake, while you was home to-day ? " she asked, in a pleased tone ; and Mrs. Crowe acknowledged such a gratifying piece of thoughtfulness for this humble friend who denied herself all luxuries. Sarah Ann brewed a generous cup of tea, and the watchers drew their chairs up to the table presently, and quelled their hunger with good country appetites. Sister Bin-son put a spoon into a small, old-fashioned glass of preserved quince, and passed it to

her friend. She was most familiar with the house, and played the part of hostess. " Spread some o' this on your bread and butter," she said to Mrs. Crowe. " Tempy wanted me to use some three or four times, but I never felt to. I know she 'd like to have us comfortable now, and would urge us to make a good supper, poor dear."

"What excellent preserves she did make ! " mourned Mrs. Crowe. " None of us has got her light hand at doin' things tasty. She made the most o' everything, too. Now, she only had that one old quince- «• tree down in the far corner of the piece, but she 'd go out in the spring and tend to it, and look at it so pleasant, and kind of expect the old thorny thing into bloomin'."

"She was just the same with folks," said Sarah Ann. " And she 'd never git more 'n a little apernful o' quinces, but she 'd have every mite o' goodness out o' those, and set the glasses up onto her best-room closet shelf, so pleased. 'T wa'n't but a week ago to-morrow mornin' I fetched her a little taste o' jelly in a teaspoon ; and she says ' Thank ye,' and took it, an' the minute she tasted it she looked up at me as worried as could be. ' Oh, I don't want to eat that,' says she.

'I always keep that in case o' sid ' You 're goin' to have the good o' one tumbler yourself,' says I. ' I 'd just like to know who's sick now, if you ain't!' An' sin-could n't help laughin', I spoke up so smart. Oh, dear me, how I shall miss talkin' over tilings with her ! She always sensed things, and got just the p'int you meant."

" She did n't begin to age until two or three years ago, did she ?" asked Mrs. Crowe. " I never saw anybody keep her looks as Tempy did. She looked young long after I begun to feel like an old woman. The doctor used to say 't was her young heart, and I don't know but what he was right. How she did do for other folks! There was one spell sho was n't at home a day to a fortnight. She got most of her livin' so, and that made her own potatoes and things last her through. None o' the young folks could get married without her, and all the old ones was disappointed if she wa'n't round when they was down with sickness and had to go. An' clean in', or tailorin' for boys, or rug-hookin', — there was nothin' but what she could do as handy as most. * I do love to work,' — ain't you heard her say that twenty times a week ? "'

Sarah Ann Binson nodded, and began to clear away the empty plates. "We may want a taste o' somethin' more towards mornin'," she said. " There 's plenty in the closet here; and in case some comes from a distance to the funeral, we '11 have a little table spread after we get back to the house."

" Yes, I was busy all the mornin'. I 've cooked up a sight o' things to bring over," said Mrs. Crowe. " I felt 't was the last I could do for her."

They drew their chairs near the stove again, and took up their work. Sister Bin-son's rocking-chair creaked as she rocked ; the brook sounded louder than ever. It was more lonely when nobody spoke, and presently Mrs. Crowe returned to her thoughts of growing old.

" Yes, Tempy aged all of a sudden. I remember I asked her if she felt as well as common, one day, and she laughed at me good. There, when Mr. Crowe begun to look old, I could n't help feeling as if somethin' ailed him, and like as not 'twas somethin' he was goin' to git right over, and I dosed him for it stiddy, half of one summer."

" How many things we shall be wanting to ask Tempy!" exclaimed Sarah Ann Binson, after a long pause. " I can't make up my mind to doin' without her. I wish ^/ folks could come back just once, and tell us how 'tis where they've gone. Seems then we could do without 'em better."

The brook hurried on, the wind blew about the house now and then ; the house itself was a silent place, and the supper, the warm fire, and an absence of any new topics for conversation made the watchers drowsy. Sister Binson closed her eyes first, to rest them for a minute; and Mrs. Crowe glanced at her compassionately, with a new sympathy for the hard-worked little woman. She made up her mind to let Sarah Ann have a good rest, while she kept watch alone; but in a few minutes her own knitting was dropped, and she, too, fell asleep. Overhead, the pale shape of Tempy Dent, the outworn body of that generous, loving-xliearted, simple soul, slept on also in its white raiment. Perhaps Tempy herself stood near, and saw her own life and its surroundings with new understanding. Perhaps she herself was the only watcher.

Later, by some hours, Sarah Ann Binson woke with a start. There was a pale light of dawn outside the small windows. Inside the kitchen, the lamp burned dim. Mrs. Crowe awoke, too.

"I think Tempy'd be the first to say 'twas just as well we both had some rest," she said, not without a guilty feeling.

Her companion went to the outer door, and opened it wide. The fresh air was none too cold, and the brook's voice was not nearly so loud as it had been in the midnight darkness. She could see the shapes of the hills, and the great shadows that lay across the lower country. The east was fast growing bright.

"'Twill be a beautiful day for the funeral," she said, and turned again, with a sigh, to follow Mrs. Crowe up the stairs.

THE DULHAM LADIES.

To be leaders of society in the town of Dulham was as satisfactory to Miss Dobin and Miss Lucinda Dobin as if Dulham were London itself. Of late years, though they would not allow themselves to suspect such treason, the most ill-bred of the younger people in the village made fun of them behind their backs, and laughed at their treasured summer mantillas, their mincing steps, and the shape of their parasols.

They were always conscious of the fact that they were the daughters of a once eminent Dulham minister; but beside this unanswerable claim to the respect of the First Pai-ish, they were aware that their mother's social position was one of superior altitude. Madam Dobin's grandmother was a Green-aple of Boston. In her younger days she had often visited her relatives, the Greenaples and Hightrees, and in seasons of festivity she could relate to a select and properly excited audience her delightful experiences of town life. Nothing could be finer than her account of having taken tea at Governor Clovenfoot's, on Beacon Street, in company with an English lord, who was indulging himself in a brief vacation from his arduous duties at the Court of St. James.

" He exclaimed that he had seldom seen in England so beautiful and intelligent a company of ladies," Madam Dobin would always say in conclusion. " He was decorated with the blue ribbon of the Knights of the Garter." 1 Miss Dobin and Miss Lu-cinda thought for many years that this famous blue ribbon was tied about the noble gentleman's leg. One day they even discussed the question openly; Miss Dobiu placing the decoration at his knee, and Miss Lucinda locating it much lower down, according to the length of the short gray socks with which she was familiar.

" You have no imagination, Lucinda," the elder sister replied impatiently. " Of course, those were the days of small-clothes and long silk stockings! " — whereat Miss Lucinda was rebuked, but not persuaded.

" I wish that my dear girls could have the outlook upon society which fell to my portion," Madam Dobin sighed, after slit-had set these ignorant minds to rights, and enriched them by communicating the final truth about the blue ribbon. " I must not chide you for the absence of opportunities, but if our cousin Harriet Greenaple were only living, you would not laek enjoyment or social education."

Madam Dobin had now been dead a great many years. She seemed an elderly woman to her daughters some time before she left them ; they thought later that she had really died comparatively young, since their own years had come to equal the record of hers. When they visited her tall white tombstone in the orderly Dulham bury ing-ground, it was a strange thought to both the daughters that they were older women than their mother had been when she died. To be sure, it was the fashion to appear older in her day, — they could remember the sober effect of really youthful married persons in cap and frisette; but, whether they owed it to the changed times or to their own qualities, they vx ielt no older themselves than ever they had. Beside upholding the ministerial dignity of their father, they were obliged to give a

lenient sanction to the ways of the world for their mother's sake ; and they combined the two duties with reverence and impartiality.

Madam Dobin was, in her prime, a walking example of refinement and courtesy. If she erred in any way, it was by keeping too strict watch and rule over her small kingdom. She acted with great dignity in all matters of social administration and etiquette, but, while it must be owned that the parishioners felt a sense of freedom for a time after her death, in their later years they praised and valued her more and more, and often lamented her generously and sincerely.

Several of her distinguished relatives attended Madam Dobin's funeral, which was long considered the most dignified and elegant pageant of that sort which had ever taken place in Dulham. It seemed to mark the close of a famous epoch in Dulham history, and it was increasingly difficult forever afterward to keep the tone of society up to the old standard. Somehow, the distinguished relatives had one by one disappeared, though they all had excellent reasons for the discontir uance of their visits.

A few had left this world altogether, an<1 the family circle of the Greenaples and Hightrees was greatly reduced in circumference. Sometimes, in summer, a stray connection drifted Dulham-ward, and was displayed to the townspeople (not to say paraded) by the gratified hostesses. It was a disappointment if the guest could not be persuaded to remain over Sunday and appear at church. When household antiquities became fashionable, the ladies remarked upon a surprising interest in their corner cupboard and best chairs, and some distant relatives revived their almost forgotten custom of paying a summer visit to Dulham. They were not long in finding out with what desperate affection Miss Dobin and v/ Miss Lucinda clung to their mother's wedding china and other inheritances, and were allowed to depart without a single teacup. One graceless descendant of the Hightrees prowled from garret to cellar, and admired the household belongings diligently, but she was not asked to accept even the dislocated cherry-wood footstool that she had discovered in the far corner of the parsonage pew. Some of the Dulham friends had always suspected that Madam Dobin made a social

misstep when she chose the Reverend Edward Dobin for her husband. She was no longer young when she married, and though she had gone through the wood and picked up a crooked stick at last, it made a great difference that her stick possessed an ecclesiastical bark. The Reverend Edward was, moreover, a respectable graduate of Harvard College, and to a woman of her standards a clergyman was by no means insignificant. It was impossible not to respect his office, at any rate, and she must have treated him with proper veneration for the sake of that, if for no other reason, though his early advantages had been insufficient, and he was quite insensible to the claims of the Green-aple pedigree, and preferred an Indian pudding to pie crust that was, without exaggeration, half a quarter high. The delicacy of Madam Dobin's touch and preference in everything, from hymns to cookery, was quite lost upon this respected preacher, yet he was not without pride or complete confidence in his own decisions.

The Reverend Mr. Dobin was never very enlightening in his discourses, and was providentially stopped short by a stroke of paralysis in the middle of his clerical career. He lived on and on through many dreary years, but his children never accepted the fact that he was a tyrant, and served him humbly and patiently. He fell at last into a condition of great incapacity and chronic trembling, but was able for nearly a quarter of a century to be carried to the meeting-house from time to time to pronounce farewell discourses. On high days of the church he was always placed in the pulpit, and held up his shaking hands when the benediction was pronounced, as if the divine gift were exclusively his own, and the other minister did but say empty words. Afterward he was usually tired and displeased and hard to cope with, but there was always a proper notice taken of these too often recurring events. For old times' and for pity's sake and from natural goodness of heart, the elder parishioners rallied manfully about the Reverend Mr. Dobin ; and whoever his successor or colleague might be, the Dobins were always called the minister's folks, while the active laborer in that vineyard was only Mr. Smith or Mr. Jones, as the case might be. At last the poor old man died, to everybody's relief and astonishment; and after he was properly preached about and

lamented, his daughters, Miss Dobin and Miss Luciuda, took a good look at life from a new standpoint, and decided that, now they were no longer constrained by home duties, they must make themselves of a great deal more use to the town.

Sometimes there is such a household as this (which has been perhaps too minutely described), where the parents linger until their children are far past middle age, and always keep them in a too childish and unworthy state of subjection. The Misses Dobin's characters were much influenced by such an unnatural prolongation of the filial relationship, and they were amazingly slow to suspect that they were not so young as they used to be. There was nothing to measure themselves by but Dulham people and things. The elm-trees were growing yet, and many of the ladies of the First Parish were older than they, and called them, with pleasant familiarity, the Dobin girls. These elderly persons seemed really to be growing old, and Miss Lucinda frequently lamented the change in society; she thought it a freak of nature and too sudden blighting of earthly hopes that several charming old friends of her mother's were no longer living. They

were advanced in age when Miss Lucimla was a young girl, though time and spurt- arc but relative, after all.

Their influence upon society would have made a great difference in many ways. Certainly, the new parishioners, who had often enough been instructed to pronounce their pastor's name as if it were spelled with one " b," would not have boldly returned again and again to their obnoxious habit of saying Dobbin. Miss Luciuda might carefully speak to the neighbor and new-comers of " my sister, Miss Do-bin ;" only the select v/ company of intimates followed her lead, and at last there was something humiliating about it, even though many persons spoke of them only as " the ladies."

" The name was originally D'Aubigne, we think," Miss Lucinda would say coldly and patiently, as if she had already explained this foolish mistake a thousand times too often. It was like the sorrows in many a provincial chateau in the lleign of Terror. The ladies looked on with increasing dismay at the retrogression in society. They felt as if they were a feeble garri-J son, to whose lot it had fallen to repul.-e a noisy, irreverent mob, an increasing band of

marauders who would overthrow all landmarks of the past, all etiquette and sgcial rank. The new minister himself was a round-faced, unspiritual-looking young man, whom they would have instinctively ignored if he had not been a minister. The new people who came to Dulham were not like the older residents, and they had no desire to be taught better. Little they cared about the Greenaples or the Hightrees ; and once, when Miss Dobin essayed to speak of some detail of her mother's brilliant experiences in Boston high life, she was interrupted, and the new-comer who sat next her at the parish sewing society began to talk about something else. We cannot believe that it could have been the tea-party at Governor Clovenfoot's which the rude creature so disrespectfully ignored, but some persons are capable of showing any lack of good taste.

The ladies had an unusual and most painful sense of failure, as they went home together that evening. " I have always made it my object to improve and interest the people at such times ; it would seem so possible to elevate their thoughts and direct them into higher channels," said Miss Dobin sadly. " But as for that Woolden woman,
there is no use in casting pearls before swine !"

Miss Lucinda murmured an indignant assent. She had a secret suspicion that the "VVoolden woman had heard the story in question oftener than had pleased her. She was but an ignorant creature; though she had lived in Dulhani twelve or thirteen years, she was no better than when she came. The mistake was in treating sister Harriet as if she were on a level with the rest of the company. Miss Lucinda had observed more than once, lately, that her sister sometimes repeated herself, unconsciously, a little oftener than was agreeable. Perhaps they were getting a trifle dull; towards spring it might be well to pass a few days with some of their friends, and have a change.

" If I have tried to do anything," said Miss Dobin in an icy tone, " it has been to stand firm in my lot and place, and to hold the standard of cultivated mind and elegant manners as high as possible. You would think it had been a hundred years since our mother's death, so completely has the effect of her good breeding and exquisite hospitality been lost sight of, here in Dulham. I could wish that our father had chosen to settle in a larger and more appreciative place. They would like to put us on the shelf, too. I can see that plainly."

" I am sure we have our friends," said Miss Lucinda anxiously, but with a choking voice. " We must not let them think we do not mean to keep up with the times, as we always have. I do feel as if perhaps — our hair " —

And the sad secret was out at last. Each of the sisters drew a long breath of relief at this beginning of a confession.

It was certain that they must take some steps to retrieve their lost ascendency. Public attention had that evening been called to their fast-disappearing locks, poor ladies; and Miss Luciuda felt the discomfort most, for she had been the inheritor of the High-tree hair, long and curly, and chestnut in color. There used to be a waviness about it, and sometimes pretty escaping curls, but these were gone long ago. Miss Dobin resembled her father, and her hair had not been luxui'iant, so that she was less changed by its absence than one might suppose. The straightness and thinness had increased so gradually that neither sister had quite ac-cepted the thought that other persons would particularly notice their altered appearance.

They had shrunk, with the reticence born of close family association, from speaking of the cause even to each other, when they made themselves pretty little lace and dotted muslin caps. Breakfast caps, they called them, and explained that these were universally worn in town; the young Prinn•>> of Wales originated them, or at any rate adopted them. The ladies offered no apology for keeping the breakfast caps on until bedtime, and in spite of them a forward child had just spoken, loud and shrill, an untimely question in the ears of the for once silent sewing society. " Do Miss Dob-binses wear them great caps because their heads is cold?"the little beast had said; and everybody was startled and dismayed.

Miss Dobin had never shown better her good breeding and valor, the younger sister thought.

" No, little girl," replied the stately Harriet, with a chilly smile. " I believe that our headdresses are quite in the fashion for ladies of all ages. And you must remember that it is never polite to make such personal remarks." It was after this that Miss Do-bin had been reminded of Madam Somebody's unusual headgear at the evening entertainment in Boston. Nobody but the Woolden woman could have interrupted her under such trying circumstances.

Miss Lucinda, however, was certain that the time had come for making some effort to replace her lost adornment. The child had told an unwelcome truth, but had paved the way for further action, and now was the time to suggest something that had slowly been taking shape in Miss Lucinda's mind. A young grand-nephew of their mother and his bride had passed a few days with them, two or three summers before, and the sisters had been quite shocked to find that the pretty young woman wore a row of frizzes, not originally her own, over her smooth, forehead. At the time, Miss Dobin and Miss Lucinda had spoken severely with each other of such bad taste, but now it made a great difference that the wearer of the frizzes was not only a relative by marriage and used to good society, but also that she came from town, and might be supposed to know what was proper in the way of toilet.

" I really think, sister, that we had better see about having some — arrangements, next time we go anywhere," Miss Dobin said unexpectedly, \\ith a slight tremble in her voice, just as they reached their own door. " There seems to be quite a fashion for them nowadays. For the parish's sake we ought to recognize " — and Miss Lucinda responded with instant satisfaction. She did not like to complain, but she had been troubled with neuralgic pains in her forehead on suddenly meeting the cold air. The sisters felt a new bond of sympathy in keeping this secret with and for each other; they took pains to say to several acquaintants that they were thinking of going to the next large town to do a few errands for Christmas.

A bright, sunny morning seemed to wish the ladies good-fortune. Old Hetty Downs, their faithful maid-servant and protector, looked after them in affectionate forebod ing. " Dear sakes, what devil's wiles may be played on them blessed innocents afore they 're safe home again! " she murmured, as they vanished round the corner of the street that led to the railway station.

Miss Dobin and Miss Lucinda paced discreetly side by side down the main street of Westbury. It was nothing like Boston, of course, but the noise was slightly confusing, and the passers-by sometimes roughly pushed against them. Westbury was a consequential manufacturing town, but a great convenience at times like this. The trifling Christmas gifts for their old neighbors and Sunday-school scholars were purchased and stowed away in their neat Fayal basket before the serious commission of the day was attended to. Here and there, in the shops, disreputable frizzes were displayed in unblushing effrontery, but no such vulgar shopkeeper merited the patronage of the Misses Dobin. They pretended not to observe the unattractive goods, and went their way to a low, one-storied building on a side street, where an old tradesman lived. He had been useful to the minister while he still remained upon the earth and had need of a wig, sandy in hue and increasingly sprinkled with gray, as if it kept pace with other changes of existence. But old Paley's shutters were up, and a bar of rough wood was nailed firmly across the one that had lost its fastening and would rack its feeble hinges in the wind. Old Paley had always been polite and bland ; they really had looked forward to a little chat with him; they had heard a year or two before of his wife's death, and meant to offer sympathy. His business of hair-dressing had been carried on with that of parasol and umbrella mending, and the condemned umbrella which was his sign flapped and swung in the rising wind, a tattered skeleton before the closed door. The ladies sighed and turned away ; they were beginning to feel tired; the day was long, and they had not met with any pleasures yet. " We might walk up the street a little farther," suggested Miss Lu-cinda; " that is, if you are not tired," as they stood hesitating on the corner after they had finished a short discussion of Mr. Paley's disappearance. Happily it was only a few minutes before they came to a stop together in front of a new, shining shop, where smirking waxen heads all in a row were decked with the latest fashions of wigs and frizzes. One smiling fragment of a gentleman stared so straight at Miss Lu-cinda with his black eyes that she felt quite coy and embarrassed, and was obliged to feign not to be conscious of his admiration. But Miss Dobin, after a brief delay, boldly opened the door and entered ; it was better to be sheltered in the shop than exposed to public remark as they gazed in at the win-

dows. Miss Lucinda felt her heart beat and her courage give out; she, coward like, left the transaction of their business to her sister, and turned to contemplate the back of the handsome model. It was a slight shock to find that he was not so attractive from this point of view. The wig he wore was well made all round, but his shoulders were roughly finished in a substance that looked like plain plaster of Paris.

" What can I have ze pleasure of showing you, young ladees?" asked a person who advanced ; and Miss Lucinda faced about to discover a smiling, middle-aged Frenchman, who rubbed his hands together and looked at his customers, first one and then the other, with delightful deference. He seemed a very civil nice person, the young ladies thought.

" My sister and I were thinking of buying some little arrangements to wear above the forehead." Miss Dobin explained, with pathetic dignity; but the Frenchman spared her any further words. He looked with eager interest at the bonnets, as if no lack had attracted his notice before. " Ah, yes. Je comprends ; ze high foreheads are not now ze mode. Je prefer them, tnoi, yes,

yes, but ze ladees must accept ze fashion; zay must now cover ze forehead with ze frizzes, ze bangs, you say. As you wis\ as you wis'!" and the tactful little nmn, with many shrugs and merry gestures at such girlish fancies, pulled down one box after another.

It was a great relief to find that this was no worse, to say the least, than any other shopping, though the solemnity and secrecy of the occasion were infringed upon by the great supply of " arrangements " and the loud discussion of the color of some crimps a noisy girl was buying from a young saleswoman the other side of the shop.

Miss Dobin waved aside the wares which were being displayed for her approval. " Something — more simple, if you please," — she did not like to say " older."

" But these are tres simple,'" protested the Frenchman. " We have nothing younger; " and Miss Dobin and Miss Lucinda blushed, and said no more. The Frenchman had his wn way; he persuaded them that nothing was so suitable as some conspicuous forelocks that matched their hair as it used to be. They would have given anything rather than leave their breakfast caps at home, if

they had known that their proper winter bonnets must come off. They hardly listened to the wig merchant's glib voice as Miss Dobin stood revealed before the merciless mirror at the back of the shop.

He made everything as easy as possible, the friendly creature, and the ladies were grateful to him. Besides, now that the bonnet was on again there was a great improvement in Miss Dobin's appearance. She turned to Miss Lucinda, and saw a gleam of delight in her eager countenance. " It really is very becoming. I like the way it parts over your forehead," said the younger sister, " but if it were long enough to go behind the ears" — " Non, non" entreated the Frenchman. " To make her the old woman at once would be cruelty!" And Lucinda, who was wondering how well she would look in her turn, succumbed promptly to such protestations. Yes, there was no use in being old before their time. Dulham was not quite keeping pace with the rest of the world in these days, but they need not drag behind everybody else, just because they lived there.

The price of the little arrangements was much less than the sisters expected, and the uncomfortable expense of their reverend father's \vi^s had been, it was proved, a tiling of the past. Miss Dobin treated her polite Frenchman with great courtesy; indeed, Miss Lucinda had more than once whispered to her to talk French, and as they were bowed out of the shop the gracious Bong-sure of the elder lady seemed to act like the string of a showerbath, and bring down an awesome torrent of foreign phrases upon the two guileless heads. It was impossible to reply; the ladies bowed again, however, and Miss Luciuda caught a last smile from the handsome wax countenance in the window, lie appeared to regard her with fresh approval, and she departed down the street with mincing steps.

" I feel as if anybody might look at me now, sister," said gentle Miss Lucinda. " I confess, I have really suffered sometimes, since I knew I looked so distressed."

" Yours is lighter than I thought it was in the shop," remarked Miss Dobin doubt-full\'7d 7 , but she quickly added that perhaps it would change a little. She was so perfectly satisfied with her own appearance that she could not bear to dim the pleasure of any one else. The truth remained that

she never would have let Lucinda choose that particular arrangement if she had seen it first in a good light. And Lucinda was thinking exactly the same of her companion.

" I am sure we shall have no more neuralgia," said Miss Dobin. " I am sorry we waited so long, dear," and they tripped down the main street of Westbury, confident that nobody would suspect them of being over thirty. Indeed, they felt quite girlish, and unconsciously looked sideways as they went along, to see their satisfying reflections in the windows. The great panes made excellent mirrors, with not too clear or lasting pictures of these comforted passers-by.

The Frenchman in the shop was making merry with his assistants. The two great frisettes had long been out of fashion; he had been lying in wait with them for two unsuspecting country ladies, who could be cajoled into such a purchase.

" Sister," Miss Lucinda was saying, " you know there is still an hour to wait before our train goes. Suppose we take a little longer walk down the other side of the way;" and they strolled slowly back again.

In fact, they nearly missed the train, naughty girls! Hetty would have been so worried, they assured each other, but they reached the station just in time.

" Lutie," said Miss Dobin, " put up your hand and part it from your forehead; it seems to be getting a little out of place;" and Miss Lucinda, who had just got bivath enough to speak, returned the information that Miss Dobin's was almost covering her eyebrows. They might have to trim them a little shorter; of course it could be done. The darkness was falling; they had taken an early dinner before they started, and now they were tired and hungry after the exertion of the afternoon, but the spirit of youth flamed afresh in their hearts, and they were very happy. If one's heart remains young, it is a sore trial to have the outward appearance entirely at vai-iance. It was the ladies' nature to be girlish, and found it impossible not to be grateful to the flimsy, ineffectual disguise which seemed to set them right with the world. The old conductor, who had known them for many years, looked hard at them as he took their tickets, and, being a man of humor and compassion, affected not to notice

anything remarkable in their appearance. " You ladies never mean to grow old, like the rest of us," he said gallantly, and the sisters fairly quaked with joy. Their young hearts would forever keep them truly unconscious of the cruel thievery of time.

" Bless us ! " the obnoxious Mrs. Woolden was saying, at the other end of the car. " There's the old maid Dobbinses, and they 've bought 'em some bangs. I expect they wanted to get thatched in a little before real cold weather; but don't they look just like a pair o' poodle dogs."

The little ladies descended wearily from the train. Somehow they did not enjoy a day's shopping as much as they used. They were certainly much obliged to Hetty for sending her niece's boy to meet them, with a lantern ; also for having a good warm supper ready when they came in. Hetty took a quick look at her mistresses, and returned to the kitchen. " I knew somebody would be foolin' of 'em," she assured herself angrily, but she had to laiigh. Their dear, kind faces were wrinkled and pale, and the great frizzes had lost their pretty curliness, and were hanging down, almost straight and very ugly, into the ladies' eyes. They could not

tuck tlu'in up under their caps, as they were sure might be done.

Then came a succession of rainy dnvs, and nobody visited the rejuvenated household. The frisettes looked very bright chestnut by the light of day, and it must be confessed that Miss Dobin took the scissors and shortened Miss Luciiida's half an inch, and Miss Luciuda returned the compliment quite secretly, because each thought her sister's forehead lower than her own. Their dear gray eyebrows were honestly displayed, as if it were the fashion not to have them match with wigs. Hetty at last spoke out, and begged her mistresses, as they sat at breakfast, to let her take the frizzes back and change them. Her sister's daughter worked in that very shop, and, though in the workroom, would be able to oblige them, Hetty was sure.

But the ladies looked at each other in pleased assurance, and then turned together to look at Hetty, who stood already a little apprehensive near the table, where she had just put down a plateful of srnokiug drop-cakes. The good creature really began to look old.

" They are worn very much iu town," said

Miss Dobin. " We think it was quite fortunate that the fashion came in just as our hair was growing a trifle thin. I dare say we may choose those that are a shade duller in color when these are a little past. Oh, we shall not want tea this evening, you remember, Hetty. I am glad there is likely to be such a good night for the sewing circle." And Miss Dobin and Miss Lucinda nodded and smiled.

" Oh, my sakes alive! " the troubled handmaiden groaned. " Going to the circle, be they, to be snickered at! Well, the Dobbin girls they was born, and the Dobbin girls they will remain till they die; but if they ain't innocent Christian babes to those that knows 'em well, mark me down for an irljit myself! They believe them front-pieces has set the clock back forty year or more, but if they 're pleased to think so, let 'em ! "

Away paced the Dulham ladies, late in the afternoon, to grace the parish occasion, and face the amused scrutiny of their neighbors. " I think we owe it to society to observe the fashions of the day," said Miss Lucinda. " A lady cannot afford to be unattractive. I feel now as if we were prepared for anything J"

AN ONLY SON.

IT was growing more and more uncomfortable in the room where Deacon Price had spent the greater part of a hot July morning. The sun did not shine in, for it was now directly overhead, but the glare of its reflection from the dusty village street and the white house opposite was blinding to the eyes. At least one of the three selectmen of Dalton, who were assembled in solemn conclave, looked up several times at the tops of the windows, and thought they had better see about getting some curtains.

There was more business than usual, but most of it belonged to the familiar detail of the office; there were bills to pay for the support of the town's-poor and the district schools, and, afterward, some discussion arose about a new piece of road which had been projected by a few citizens, who were as violently opposed by others. The selectmen were agreed upon this question, but they

proposed to speak in private with the county commissioners, who were expected to view the region of the new highway the next week. This, however, had been well canvassed at their last meeting, and they had reached no new conclusions since; so presently the conversation flagged a little, and Deacon Price drummed upon the ink-spattered table with his long, brown fingers, and John Kendall, the grist-miller, rose impatiently and went to the small window, where he stood with blinking eyes looking down into the street. His well-rounded figure made a pleasant shadow in that part of the room, but it seemed to grow hotter every moment. Captain Abel Stone left his chair impatiently, and taking his hat went down the short flight of stairs that led to the street, knocking his thick, shuffling boots clumsily by the way. He reached the sidewalk and looked up and down the street, but nobody was coming; so he turned to Asa Ball, the shoemaker, who was standing in his shop-door.

" Business ain't brisk, I take it ?" inquired the captain; and Mr. Ball replied that he didn't do much more than tend shop, nowadays. Folks would keep on

buying cheap shoes, and thinking they saved more money on two pair a year for five dollars than when he used to make 'em one pair for four. " But I make bettt-i pay than I used to working at my trade, and so I ain't going to fret," said Asa shrewdly, with a significant glance at a modest pile of empty cloth-boot boxes; and the captain laughed a little, and took a nibble at a piece of tobacco which he had found with much difficulty in one of his deep coat pockets. He had followed the sea in his early life, but had returned to the small, stony farm which had been the home of his childhood, perhaps fifteen years before this story begins. He had taken as kindly to inland life as if he had never once been spattered with sea water, and had been instantly given the position in town affairs which his wealth and character merited. He still retained a good deal of his nautical way of looking at things. One would say that to judge by his appearance he had been well rubbed with tar and salt, and it was supposed by his neighbors that his old sea-chests were guardians of much money ; he was overrated by some of them as being worth fifteen thousand dollars with the farm

thrown in. The captain was considered very peculiar, because he liked to live in the somewhat dilapidated little farmhouse, and some of his attempts at cultivating the sterile soil were the occasion of much amusement. He had made a large scrap-book, during his long sea-voyages, of all sorts of hints and suggestions for the tillage of the ground, gleaned from books and newspapers and almanacs, and nobody knows where else. He had pasted these in, or copied them in his stiff, careful handwriting, and pleased himself by watching his collection grow while he was looking forward through the long, storm-tossed years to his quiet anchorage among the Dalton hills. He was a single man, and though a braver never trod the quarter-deck, from motives of wisest policy he seldom opposed his will to that of Widow Martha Hawkes, who had consented to do him the great favor of keeping his house.

" Havin' a long session to-day, seems to me," observed the shoemaker, with little appearance of the curiosity which he really felt.

" There was a good many p'ints to be looked over," answered Captain Stone, becoming aware that he had secrets to guard, and looking impenetrable and unconcerned. "It's worked into a long drought, just as I said — I never took note of a drier sky ; don't seem now as if we ever should get a sprinkle out of it, but I suppose we shall; " ami he turned with a sigh to the door, and disappeared again up the narrow stairway. The three horses which were tied to adjacent posts in the full blaze of the sun all hung their ancient heads wearily, and solaced their disappointment as best they might. They had felt certain, when the captain appeared, that the selectmen's meeting was over. If they had been better acquainted with politics they might have wished that there could be a rising of the opposition, so that their masters would go out of office for as many years as they had come in.

The captain's companions looked up at him eagerly, as if they were sure that he was the herald of the expected tax-collector, who was to pay a large sum of money to them, of which the town treasury was in need. It was close upon twelve o'clock, and only a very great emergency would detain them beyond that time. They were

growing very hungry, and when the captain, after a grave shake of his head, had settled into his chair again, they all felt more or less revengeful, though Deacoii Price showed it by looking sad. One would have thought that he was waiting with reluctance to see some punishment descend upon the head of the delaying official.

" Well, Mis' Hawkes will be waiting dinner for me, and she never likes that," said Captain Stone at last; and just at that minute was heard the sound of wheels.

" Perhaps it's my mare stepping about, — she's dreadful restive in fly-time," suggested Mr. Kendall, and at once put his head out of the window; but when he took it in again, it was to tell his fellow-officers that Jackson was coming, and then they all sat solemnly in their chairs, with as much dignity as the situation of things allowed. Their judicial and governmental authority was plainly depicted in their expression. On ordinary occasions they were not remarkable, except as excellent old-fashioned countrymen; but when they represented to the world the personality and character of the town of Dalton, they would not have

looked out of place seated in that stately company which Carpaccio has painted in the .Reception of the English Embassadors. It was Dalton that gave audience that summer day, in the dusty, bare room, as Venice listens soberly in the picture.

They heard a man speak to his horse and leap to the ground heavily, and then listened eagerly to the clicks and fumblings which represented the tying of the halter, and then there were sounds of steps upon the stairway. The voice of Mr. Ball was heard, but it did not seem to have attracted much attention, and presently the long-waited-for messenger was in the room, lie was dusty and sunburnt, and looked good-naturedly at his hosts. They greeted him amiably enough, and after he put his worn red handkerchief away he took a leather wallet from his pocket, and looking at a little roll of bills almost reluctantly turned them over with lingering fingers and passed them to Mr. Kendall, who sat nearest him, saying that he believed it was just right.

There was little else said, and after the money had again been counted the meeting was over. There was indeed a hurried arrangement as to who should guard

AN ONLY

the treasury, but when Deacon Price acknowledged that he meant to go to South Dalton next morning, he was at once deputed to cany the remittance to the bank there, where the town's funds and many of its papers already reposed. The deacon said slowly that he did n't know as he cared about keeping so much money in the house, but he was not relieved by either of his colleagues, and so these honest men separated and returned to private life again. Their homes were at some distance from each other; but for a half mile or so Deacon Price followed Captain

Stone, and a cloud of dust followed them both. Then the captain turned to the left, up toward the hills; but Deacon Price kept on for some distance through the level lands, and at last went down a long lane, unshaded except here and there where some ambitious fence stakes had succeeded in changing themselves into slender willow-trees. In the spring the sides of the lane had been wet, and were full of green things, growing as fast as they could; but now these had been for some time dried up. The lane was bordered with dusty mayweed, and three deep furrows were worn through the

turf, where the wagon wheels and the horse's patient feet had traveled back and forward so many years. The house stood at the end, looking toward the main road as if it wished it were there; it was a low-storied white house, with faded green blinds.

The deacon had tried to hurry his slow horse still more after he caught sight of another horse and wagon standing in the wide dooryard. He had entirely forgotten, until that moment, that his niece and housekeeper, Eliza Storrow, had made a final announcement in the morning that she was going to start early that afternoon for the next town to help celebrate a golden wedding. Poor Eliza had been somewhat irate because even this uncommon season of high festival failed to excite her uncle's love for society. She made him run the gauntlet, as usual on such occasions, by telling him successively that he took no interest in nobody and nothing, and that she was sure she should n't know what to say when people asked where he was ; that it looked real unfeeling and cold-hearted, and he couldn't expect folks to show any interest in him. These arguments, with many others, had been brought

forward on previous occasions until the deacon knew them all by heart, and he listened to them impassively that morning, only observing cautiously to his son that Eliza must go through with just so much. But he promised to come back early from the village, since Eliza and the cousin who was to call for her meant to start soon after twelve. It was a long drive, and they wished to be in good season for the gathering of the clans.

He left the horse standing in the yard and went into the house, feeling carefully at his inner coat pocket as he did so. Eliza had been watching for him, but the minute he came in sight she had left the window and begun to scurry about in the pantry. The deacon did not stop to speak to her, but went directly to his bedroom, and after a moment's thought placed the precious wallet deep under the pillows. This act was followed by another moment's reflection, and as the old man turned, his son stood before him in the doorway. Neither spoke; there was a feeling of embarrassment which was not uncommon between them ; but presently the young man said, " Eliza's been waiting for you to have your dinner; she 's in a great

hurry to get off. I be in just as quick as I take care of the horse."

" You let her be ; I put her up myself," said the deacon a little ungraciously. " I guess Eliza'll get there soon enough. I should n't think she 'd want to start to ride way over there right in the middle of the day." At another time he would have been pleased with Warren's offer of aid, for that young man's bent was not in what we are pleased to call a practical direction. As he left the kitchen he noticed for the first time Mrs. Starbird, who sat by the farther window dressed in her best, and evidently brimming over with reproachful impatience. Deacon Price was a hospitable man, and stopped to shake hands with her kindly, and to explain that he had been delayed by some business that had come before the selectmen. He was politely assured that the delay was not of the least consequence, for Mrs. Starbird was going to drive the colt, and could make up the lost time on the road. As they stood talking, Eliza's footsteps were heard behind them, and, without turning or deigning to enter into any conversation with his niece, the deacon went out into the bright sunlight again.

Warren had preceded him after all, and was unfastening one of the traces, and his father unbuckled the other without a word. " You go in and have your dinner, — why won't you, father ? " the young man said, looking up appealingly. " You need n't be afraid but I '11 do this all right."

" I declare, I was grieved when I saw, as I come up the lane, that you had n't mended up the fence there where I told you this forenoon. I had to be off, and there's the two calves right into the garden piece, and I don't know what works they 've been and done. It does seem too bad, Warren."

The son had worn a pleased and almost triumphant look, as if he had good news to tell, but now his face fell, and he turned crimson with shame and anger. " I would n't have forgot that for anything! " he stammered. " I 've been hurrying as fast as I could with something I 've been doing. I 'm going off " — but his father had already stepped inside the barn door with the hungry horse, and it was no use to say any more. Presently the deacon went into the house and ate his dinner, and after the few dishes had been washed, and Eliza had told him about the bread, and a piece of cold

boiled beef, and a row of blueberry pies, and the sheet of gingerbread, which she had provided for the family's sustenance in her absence, she added that she might not be back until early Wednesday morning, and then she drove away in triumph with cousin Star-bird. It was the first holiday the good woman had had for more than a year, except for church - going, and the deacon wished her good-day with real affection and sympathy, having already asked if she had everything she wanted to carry over, and finally desiring his respects to be given to the folks. He stood at the corner of the house and watched her all the way down the lane until she turned into the main road, and Eliza herself was much pleased as she caught sight of him. She waved her hand gallantly, to which he responded by an almost imperceptible inclination of the head and at once turned away.

" There ain't a better man alive," said cousin Starbird, whipping the elderly colt; " he's as set as anybody I ever see, in his own ways, but he's real good-hearted. I don't know anybody I 'd look to quicker than him if I got into misfortune. He 's aged a good deal this last year, don't you think he has, 'Liza ? Sometimes I feel sure that Warren's odd notions wears on him more than we think."

"Course they do," said Eliza, throwing back the shawl which she had felt obliged to put on at first, out of respect to the occasion. " His father's mindful of Warren every hour in the day. He is getting more and more helpless and forgitful, and uncle's growing feeble, and he ain't able either to hire help or to do the farm work himself. Sometimes Warren takes holt real good, but it ain't often; and there he sets, up in that room he 's fixed over the wood-house, and tinkers all day long. Last winter he used to be there till late at night; he took out one o' the window panes and set a funnel <3ut through, and used to keep a fire going and a bright light up there till one or two o'clock in the morning. His father never slept a wink, I don't believe. He looks like a man tjiat 's hard on to eighty, and he wa'n't but sixty-seven his last birthday. I guess Warren 's teased him out of about all the bank money he had put away. There! I used to get interested myself in Warren's notions about his machines, but now I can't bear to hear him begin, and I go right into the pantry and rattle round as if I was drove to pieces."

" I suppose his father has indulged him more, seeing that he was so much younger than all the rest of his children, and they being dead anyway. I declare, I never see such a beautiful creatur' as Warren's mother was. I always thought she was kind of homesick here; 't was a lonesome place to me, always, and I never counted on its being healthy. The deacon 's begun to look kind o' mossy, and I don't think it's all worry o' mind. It's kind of low land, and has always been called fevery." Cousin Starbird was apt to look on the dark side of things. " You can't always see the marks o' trouble," she went on. " There was old John Stacy, that lost three children in one day with scarlet fever the fall after his wife died ; then his house got afire, and the bank failed wln-rc his property was. Job himself could n't be no worse off; and he took on dreadful, as one thing after another came upon him, but there wa'n't a younger appearing man of his age anywhere at the time he died. He seemed to spring right up again, like a bent withe. I always thought it was a kind of a pity that the deacon did n't push Warren

right off while he was young. He kept him to home trying to make a farm-boy of him till he was a grown man."

" Warren used to beseech him dreadfully to let him go off, when I first come over to live," said Eliza Storrow. " He had a great notion of working in some kind of a machine shop, and they said that there wa'n't so smart a workman there as he was; but he got a notion that he could improve on one of the machines, and lost all his interest in workin' his trade, and the end of it was that he spent a sight o' money to get a patent, and found somebody had stepped in with another just the week before. It was an awful mean thing, too, for some thought it was his notion that had been stole from him. There was a fellow that boarded where he did, to Lowell, that left all of a sudden, and they thought he took the plan, — Warren being always free and pleasant with him, — and then let somebody else have part of it to get the patent through ; anyway it was n't called for in any name they knew. Warren was dreadful discouraged about it, and was set against folks knowing, so don't you never say nothing that I said about it. I think he's kind of crazed about machin-

ery, and I don't believe he knows what he 's about more than half the time. He never give me a misbeholden word, I '11 say that for him, but it's getting to be a melancholy habitation if ever I see one," said Eliza mournfully ; and after this the conversation turned to more hopeful themes relating to the golden wedding.

The deacon had sighed as he turned away. He wondered if they would make the twelve-mile journey in safety, and smiled in spite of himself as he remembered an old story. He wished he had reminded them of those two old women who were traveling from Dalton to Somerset, and forgot where they came from, and what their names were, and where they were going. After this hidden spring of humor had bubbled to the surface, a little too late for anybody's enjoyment but his own, he relapsed into his usual plaintive gravity, and, bringing a hammer and nails and some stakes from the wood-house, he went out to mend the broken fence. It had been so often patched and propped that it now seemed hardly to be repaired again. The boards and posts had rotted away, and the gamesome calves had forced a wide breach in so weak a wall. It was a

half afternoon's work, and the day was hot, but the tired old man set about it unflinchingly, and took no rest until he had given the topmost rail a shake and assured him, self that it would last through his day. He had brought luore tools and pieces of board, and he put these together to be replaced. Just as he began his work he caught sight of his son walking quickly away, far beyond the house, across the pastures. The deacon gave a heavy sigh, and as he hammered and sawed and built his fence again, there had been more than one sigh to follow it, for was not this only f.on more strange and helpless and useless than ever? There seemed little to look forward to in life.

The garden was being sadly treated and hindered by the drought: the beets and onions were only half grown, and the reliable old herb-bed seemed to have given up the fight altogether. In one place there had once been a flower-bed which belonged to Warren's mother, but it was almost wholly covered with grass. Eliza had no fondness for flowers, and the two men usually were unconscious that there were such things in the world. But this afternoon the deacon

was glad to see a solitary sprig of London Pride, which stood out in bold relief against the gray post by the little garden gate. It sent a bright ray of encouragement into the shadow of his thoughts, and he went on his way cheerfully. He told himnelf that next he would attend to the wagon wheels, because he should need to start early in the morning, in order to get home before the heat of the day ; it was a hot piece of road from here to the south village. He wondered idly where Warren had gone ; he was glad he had not asked for money that day, but he had done questioning his son about his plans, or even the reason of his occasional absences.

The side door, which led into the kitchen, was shaded now, and a westerly breeze was coming across the level fields^ so the deacon sat down on the doorstep to rest. The old cat came out as if she wished for company, and rubbed against his arm and mewed without making any noticeable sound. She put her fore-feet on the old man's knee and looked eagerly in his face and mewed again inaudibly, and her master laughed and wondered what she wanted. 4i I suppose the cellar door is locked and bolted, and you

wanfc to go down," said the deacon, " that's it, ain't it? I should ha' thought 'Liza would have rec'lected about them kittens, should n't you ? " and pleasing himself with the creature's companionship, he rose and entered the house. The cat trotted alongside and disappeared quickly down the stairway, and, moved by some strange impulse, Deacon Price went into his bedroom to make sure that the wallet was safe under the pillow. He did not reach it at first, and he groped again, thinking that he had forgotten he pushed it so far under. But although he eagerly threw off the clothes and the pillows, and shook them twice over, and got down on his hands and knees and crept under the bed, and felt an odd singing noise grow louder and louder in his head, and at last became dizzy and dropped into the nearest chair, there was no wallet to be found.

Then he crept out into the empty kitchen, where the only sound was made by a fly that buzzed dismally in a spider's web. The air was close and hot in the house, and as the old man stood in the doorway it seemed as if there had some change come over his whole familiar world. He felt puzzled and weak, and at first started to go out

to the wagon with the vain hope of finding the lost purse ; it might be that he — But there was no use in imagining that he had done anything but put it carefully under the pillow, that his son had stood in the doorway as he lifted his head, and that the money was gone. It was no use to deceive himself, or to hunt through the house ; he had always before his eyes the picture of the pasture slope with the well-known figure of his son following the path that led across it to the nearest railroad station, a mile or two away.

The daylight waned slowly, and the heat ^ of the sun lingered late into the night. Poor John Price went through with his usual duties mechanically, but with perfect can-, and made the doing of his work last as long as he could. The pig and the chickens and the horse were fed ; then there were the cows to bring in from pasture and to be milked ; and at last the poor man even remembered the cat, and gave her a saucer of milk for her supper ; but still it would not grow dark, and still the shame and sorrow weighed him down. In his restlessness he went through the lower rooms of the house, and opened the front door and shut it again,

and looked into the stiff little best room, and felt as if he were following the country custom, so familiar to him, of watching with the dead.

He did not get much sleep that night, in the uncomfortable bed which he tried to put into some sort of order before he lay down. Once he prayed aloud that the Lord would vouchsafe him a miracle, and that he might find his trust again, and what was still more precious, his confidence in his only son. For some reason he could not bear the sound of his own voice ; and the thought of his time-honored office in the church pained him, for was it not disgraced and made a reproach ?

Little by little the first sharpness of the shock wore away, while he tried to think what was to be done. The thought seized him that his son might have left some explanation of his going away, and he rose and took a candle and went to the little work-shop. There was less than the usual litter of cog-wheels and springs and screws, but somehow in the hot little room a feeling of reassurance and almost of hope took possession of him. It might be that Warren's hopes would not be disappointed, that he might be able to repay the stolen sum, that

he had only secreted it, and would return later and give it back ; for the poor deacon assured himself over and over that he would talk about the boy's affairs with him, and try again to aid him and to put him into a likely way at last, even if he had to mortgage the farm.

But in the morning, if there were still no signs of the lad, what could be done ? The money which Jerry Jackson had owed the town as tax-collector, and paid at last that very day, — that seven hundred dollars ; the five hundred dollar bill, and the two that stood for a hundred each, and some smaller bills which were to pay the interest, — how should they be replaced? He had no ready money of any amount, nor would have until the pay came for some hay, or unless he could persuade a neighbor, whose payments were honest but slow, to take up a note given for a piece of outlying woodland sold the winter before.

All through that long summer night he worried and waited for the morning, and sometimes told himself that his only son had robbed him, and sometimes said that Warren would never serve him like that, and when he came home it would be all made

right. The whippoorwills were singing about the house, and one even came to perch on the kitchen doorstep and repeat its accusing cr£. The waning moon rose late, and made a solemn red light in the east, and shone straight in at the little bedroom window as if it were a distant bale-fire on the hills. A little dog kept up a fierce barking by the next farmhouse, far away across the fields, and at last the tired man was ready to think his miserable wakefulness was the fault of the cur. . . . Yes, he had given Warren all the money he could, he had meant well by the boy, and surely now, unless the poor fellow had gone mad, there would be some way out of all this trouble ; at any rate, he would not let other people have a chance to call his son a thief until there was no help for it. The next morning, after a short, uneasy sleep, from which the deacon had a sad awaking, he hungrily ate some breakfast at the pantry shelves, and harnessed the old horse, and set out on a day's journey of which he hardly knew the end. He shut the door of the house and locked it, and gave a look of lingering affection at the old place, even stopping the horse for a minute in the lane that he might turn to survey it

again most carefully. He felt as if he were going to do it wrong, and as if it were a conscious thing, the old weather-beaten dwelling that had sheltered him all his life, and those who had been dearest to him. It had no great attractions for a stranger. It was a representative house for that somewhat primitive farming region, though it had fallen out of repair, and wore a damaged and re-sourceless aspect. The appearance of a man's home is exactly characteristic of him-\s self. Human nature is more powerful than its surroundings, and shapes them inevitably to itself.

It was still very early in the morning, and few persons were stirring. In fact, Deacon Price met nobody on the road except a sleepy boy following his cows to pasture, and he did not feel like looking him in the face, but gave a pull at the reins to hurry the horse and pass by without question. He took a cross road that was cool and shady at that hour, and while he journeyed slowly up the rough by-way he let the horse choose its own course without guidance. Some birds were crying and calling in the woods close by, as if it were altogether a day of ill omen and disaster. John Price

felt more and more as if his world was coming to an end, and everything was going to pieces. He never had understood his son very well; there are some people who are like the moon, with one side always hidden and turned away, and Warren was only half familiar to his father. The old man had been at first inclined to treat his bright boy with a sort of respect and reverence, but in later years this had changed little by little to impatience and suspicion. It had been a great mortification that he had been obliged to maintain him, and once when somebody, perhaps Eliza Storrow, had been commenting upon a certain crop of wild oats which a neighboring lad had arranged for his harvesting, the deacon was heard to mutter, " Better them than no crop at all! " Yet he had never suffered his acquaintances to comment upon his son's behavior; his own treatment of him in public had insisted upon the rendering of respect from other people, but he had not acknowledged to himself, until this last sad night, that there was no practical result to be hoped for from Warren's gifts and graces. This might have been borne, and they might have struggled on together, somehow or other, but for this terri-

ble blow of the theft of the town's money, which now left a debt and sorrow on the old man's shoulders almost too heavy to be borne.

In a short time the woods were passed, and the road led out to a pleasant country of quite different character from the lowland neighborhood left behind. There were gently sloping hills and long lines of elms, and the farms looked more prosperous. One farm only on this road was unproductive, and this was partly the fault of art, and partly of nature, for it was the homestead of Captain Stone, a better sailor than farmer. Its pastures were gathering-places for the ledges, and the fields were all made swampy by many springs. It seemed to be the waste corner of that region for all unused and undeveloped materials of farming land ; but while there was every requisite, there was a chaotic and primitive arrangement of clay, rock, and sand. Yet the captain had settled down here in blissful content as a tiller of the soil; and while he might have bought the best farm in the county, he congratulated himself upon his rare privileges here, and would have found more level and kindly acres as uninteresting as being becalmed in

tropic seas. He worked his farm as he had sailed his ships, by using tact and discretion, and with true seaman's philosophy he never fretted. He waited for the wind to change, or the tide of spring to flow, or of winter to ebb, for he had long ago learned there was no hurrying nature; and to hear him talk of one of his small plots of thin hay, or slow-growing potatoes, you would have thought it an intelligent creature which existed mainly on his benevolent encouragement and tolerance. By some persons the captain was laughed at, and by others he was condemned. The trouble was that he had a shrewd insight into human nature, and was so impossible to deceive or to persuade against his will that he had made many enemies, who had hoped to grow rich by emptying the good old man's pockets.

It was to this lifelong friend that Deacon Price had turned in his extremity; but as he drew nearer that morning to the red house on the hilltop, his heart began to fail him, for what if he should be refused! There seemed no other resource, in such a case, but to make the sad occurence known, or to go away in search of Warren himself. He could put the deeds of his farm, those

worn deeds that had come down from father to son, generation after generation, into the hands of the other selectmen, who would be sure to stand his friends and keep the secret for a time. Warren had looked discouraged, and pale, and desperate in the last mouth, and his father suddenly remembered this, and groaned aloud as he wished that the boy had come to him, and that he had made it possi-/ ble, instead of coldly ignoring and disapproving him day after day; such a mixture of wrath and shame and compassion has seldom been in a father's heart.

The captain was abroad early, and the deacon saw him first, sauntering about at the foot of the slope on which his house and buildings stood. He seemed to be examining the soil, and greeted his guest with a hearty satisfaction. The deacon slowly alighted, and leaving his trusty steed to gnaw the fence or browse among the bushes as she chose, went into the field. He walked feebly, and when he met the captain he could hardly find words to tell his errand. Men of his kind are apt to be made silent by any great occurrence ; they have rarely \'7d anything but a limited power of expression,

and their language only serves them for common use. Those who have lived close to nature understand each other without speech, as dogs or horses do, and the elder generations of New Englanders knew less of society and human companionship and association than we can comprehend.

The captain watched his visitor as he came toward him, and when they met he gave one quick, final look, and then proceeded to make use of his usual forms of greeting, as if he had no idea that anything was the matter.

" I 've taken a notion to set out some cramb'ries hereabouts another year," he announced. "I never made a voyage to sea without cramb'ries aboard, if I could help myself. They last well, and taste sprightly when other things is begun to lose savor. I don't cut any hay to speak of, in this piece. I 've been meaning to tackle it somehow — See here," — pushing it with his great foot, — " it's all coming up brakes and sedge. I do' know 's you want to be standing about — It is master spongy for good grass land, and 't would be a great expense to drain it off. I s'pose I 'in gettin' too old to try any of these new notions, but

they sort of divert me. We're having a bad spell o' drought, ain't we? 'T is all tops of rocks about here, and we 're singed pretty brown." The captain chattered more briskly than was his wont; it was impossible to mistake the fact of his being a sailor, for indeed that business stamps its followers with an unmistakable brand.

They ventured upon a wetter spot than usual, and when the deacon pulled up his foot from the mire underneath with a resounding plop, his host proposed that they should seek the higher ground.

" Pretty smart at home ? '" asked the captain presently, to end a season of strange silence; and the deacon replied, at first somewhat sorrowfully, that they were fair to middling, but explained directly that Eliza was away for a couple of nights, and AYunx-n too ; it cost a great effort to speak the young man's name.

" Oh, yes, I rec'lect," growled the captain amiably. "You spoke about the golden weddin' yesterday; I should thought you 'd ha' gone too, along with 'Liza; such junkets ain't to be had every day. I must say I wish something or other would happen to take Mis' Hawkes's attention off of me,"

dropping his voice cautiously, as they came nearer to the house. " She 's had a dreadful grumpy time of it, this week past, and looked homely enough to stop a clock. I used to be concerned along in the first of it, when I come off the sea, but I found it did n't do no hurt, and so I let her work, and first thing you know the wind is veered round again handsome, and off you go."

The deacon tried to laugh at this; the friends seated themselves on the off side of the wood-pile, under the shade of a great choke-pear tree. They had mounted the chopping-block, which was a stout elm log, standing on six legs, so that it looked like some stupid, blunderheaded creature of not altogether harmless disposition. The two old men were quite at its mercy if it should canter away suddenly; but they talked for some minutes on ordinary subjects, and even left their position to go to inspect the pigs, and returned again, before the deacon arrived at an explanation of his errand.

It was a hard thing to do, and the captain turned and looked at him narrowly.

" I 've got to use the money right away as soon as I can have it. I want to see to some business this forenoon ; you know I 've

been calc'latin' to go to the south village to-day anyway. I did n't know for certain I should have to see about this, or I would n't have given you such short notice " — and here the deacon stopped again ; it had come very near an untruth, this last sentence, and he would not cheat the man of whom he was asking so great a favor.

" I did n't fetch the papers along because I did n't know how 't would be with you," he explained; " they '11 make you safe. Austin's folks was talking round, this spring, to see if I wanted to part with our north field; his youngest son's a smart fellow, and wants to set up for himself and have a truck farm. But I'm only asking the loan for a time, ye know, neighbor." and the deacon looked anxiously at the old captain, and then leaned over, poking the chips about with the butt of his whip, which he had brought with him from the wagon.

" You shall have it," said the captain at last. " 'T ain't everybody I 'd do such a thing to obleege, and I am only going to have my say about one thing, John : I never had no family of ray own, and I suppose the feelin's of a father are somethin' I don't know nothing about, for or against; but I

must say I hate to see ye an old man before your time, runnin' all out and looking discouraged on account o' favoriu' Warren. You 11 come in astern o' the lighter, and he too; and if he 's been beseechin' ye to get this money together to further his notions, I 'm doing ye both a wrong to let ye have it. But I can't deny ye, and I 've got more than what ye say ye want, right here in the house as it happens. I was going to buy into that new three-masted schooner the Otises have got on the stocks now; I don't know but I am getting along in years to take hold of anything new in navigation."

" I ain't intending to let Warren have none o' this," said the deacon humbly, and he longed to say more, and felt as if he never could hold up his head again among his fellows; and the time seemed very long and dreary before the captain came back from his house with the note ready to sign, and the seven hundred dollars ready to place in the deacon's gray and shaking hand. His benefactor pondered long over this strange visit, longing to know what had happened, but he assured himself over and over that he could n't help letting him have it, and if never a cent of it came back there

was nobody he was gladder to oblige. And John Price took his weary way to the south village of Dalton, and paid a sum of seven hundred and thirty-five dollars to the creditors of the town. It was not until early in the afternoon that old Abel Stone suddenly bethought himself that something might have happened about that payment of Jerry Jackson's. If he were not growing old and a fool at last! Why had n't he asked the deacon if he had lost the money he had taken home from the selectmen's office! And when Mrs. Hawkes afterward ventured to ask him a harmless question, he had grown red in the face and poured forth a torrent of nautical language which had nearly taken her breath away, without apparent reason or excuse. The captain, it must be confessed, was an uncommon swearer; he was one of the people who seem to serve as volcanoes, or outlets for the concealed anger of poor human nature. It is difficult to explain why profanity seems so much more unlawful and shocking in some persons than in others, but there was something fairly amusing in the flurry and sputter of irreverent words which betokened excitement of any kind in the mind of Cap-

tain Stone. He even forgot himself so far as to swear a little occasionally in the course of earnest exhortations in the evening prayer-meetings. There was not a better man or a sincerer Christian in the town of Dalton, though he had become a church-member late in life; and knowing this, there was never anything but a compassionate smile when he grew red in the face with zeal, and recommended the poor damned dogs of heathen to mercy.

Nothing seemed to have changed outwardly at the south village. John Price did his errands and finished his business as quickly as possible, and avoided meeting his acquaintances, for he could not help fearing that he should be questioned about this miserable trouble. As he left the bank he could not help giving a sigh of relief, for that emergency was bridged over ; and for a few minutes he kept himself by main force from looking at the future, or asking himself " What next ? "

But as he turned into his dust-powdered lane again at noon, the curious little faces of the mayweed blossoms seemed to stare up at him, and there was nobody to speak to him,

and the house was like a tomb where all the years of his past were lying dead, and all the pleasantness of life existed only in remembrance.

He began to wish for Warren in an unexpected way; and as he looked about the house he saw everywhere some evidence of his son's mechanical skill. Had not Eliza Storrow left home without a fear because, as she always said, Warren was as handy as a woman ? The remembrance of such patient diligence at his own chosen work, his quietness under reproof, his evident discomfort at having to be dependent upon his father, linked to a perfect faith in the ultimate success of his plans, — the thought of all these things flashed through the old man's mind. " I wish I had waited 'til he told me what he had to say, yisterday," said Deacon Price to himself. " 'T was strange about that fence too. He 's al'ays been willing to take holt and help whenever I spoke to him." He even came to believe that the boy had grown desperate, and in some emergency had gone in search of new materials for his machine. " He 's so forgitful," said the father, " he may have forgot to speak about the money, and 't was but a small-looking roll of bills.

He '11 be back to-night, like's not, as concerned as can be when he finds out what't was he took." It was the way we remember only the good qualities of our friends who have died, and let the bad ones fade out of sight, and so know the angels that were growing in them all the while, and have thrown off the disguise and hindrance of the human shape.

Towards evening Jacob Austin, a neighbor, came into the yard on an errand, and was astonished to see how tired and old the deacon looked. He had left the oxen and their great load of coarse meadow hay standing in the road at the end of the lane, and meant at first to shoulder the borrowed pitchfork and quickly rejoin them, but it was impossible. He asked if anything were the matter, and was answered that there was something trying about such a long spell of drought, which did not in the least satisfy his curiosity.

" No," said the deacon, " I 'm getting to be an old man, but I keep my health fairly. Eliza and Warren, they 're both off 'tending to their own concerns, but I make sure one or both of 'm '11 be back toward sundown." And Jacob, after casting about in his mind

for anything further to say, mentioned again that 't was inconvenient to break a pitchfork right in the middle of loading a rack, and went away.

" Looked to me as if he had had a stroke," he told his family that night at supper-time;

and the conduct of Warren and Eliza Stor-row, in going off and leaving the old deacon to shift for himself, was most severely commented upon.

But all this time, the latter half of that Tuesday afternoon, Eliza and her cousin Starbird were jogging toward home over the Dalton and Somerset hills. The colt was in good trim, and glad to be nearing his own familiar stall again, and struck out at an uncommonly good pace, though none of the swiftest at that. It was hardly six o'clock when the two tired-out and severely sunburnt women came into the yard. The deacon heard the high-pitched voice which he knew so well, before he heard the sound of the wheels on the soft, dry turf, and went out to greet the new-comers, half glad and half afraid. Eliza took it for granted that Warren was either in the workshop as usual, or, as she scornfully expressed it, roaming the hills, and did not ask for him. Cousin

Starbird had accepted an invitation to tea, as her home was three miles farther on. They were both heavy women, and stiff from sitting still so long in the old wagon, and they grumbled a little as they walked toward the house.

" Yes, 't was a splendid occasion," Eliza answered the deacon, as he stood near, hitching the colt to a much gnawed post. " It all went off beautifully. Everybody wanted to know where you was, an' Warren. There, we talked till we was all about dead, and eat ourselves sick ; you never saw a handsomer table in your life. The old folks stood it well, but I see they 'd begun to kind o' give out at dinner-time to-day, — last night was the celebration, you know, because some could come in the evenin' that was occupied by day. They wanted us to stop longer, but I see't was best to break it up, and I 'd rather go over again by an' by, and spend the day in peace an' quietness, and have a good visit. We 've been saying, as we rode along, that we should n't be surprised if the old folks kind o' faded out after this, they 've been lookin' forward to it so long. Well, it's all over, like a hoss-race; " and Eliza heaved a great sigh and went into the front room to

open the blinds and make it less stuffy; then she removed her best bonnet in her own room, and presently came out to get tea, dressed in her familiar everyday calico gown.

The deacon was sitting by the open window, drumming on the sill; he had a trick of beating a slow tattoo with the ends of his queerly shaped fingers. They were long and dry, and somehow did not look as if they were useful, though John Price had been a hard-working man. Cousin Starbird had come downstairs first, and had gone out to find a piece of the golden wedding cake that had been left in the wagon. Eliza was busy in the pantry, scolding a good deal at the state she found it in.

" Whatever is this great thing in my pocket! " she exclaimed, for something had struck the table-leg as she came by it to bring the last brace of blueberry pies ; then quickly fumbling in the pocket's depths she took out the deacon's great brown wallet, and presented it to its owner.

" Good King Agrippy ! ' ? said the amazed man, snatching it, and looking at Eliza angrily and then at the wallet again, and turning it over in his hand.

" I ain't give it a thought, from that minute to this," said Eliza, who was not a little frightened. " I s'pose you 've been thinking you lost it. I thought you looked dreadful wauiblecropped when I first saw you. Why, you see, I did n't undertake to wash yesterday mornin', because I did n't want the clothes a-layin' and mildewin', and I kind of thought perhaps I 'd put it off till next week, anyway, though it ain't my principle to do fortnight's washes. An' I had so much to do, gettin' ready to start, that I 'd gone in early and made up your bed and not put a clean sheet on ; but you was busy takin' out the hoss after you come home at noon, and had your dinner to eat, and I had the time to spare, so I just slipped in and stripped off the bedclothes then, and this come out from under the pillow. I meant to hand it to you when you come in from the barn, but I forgot it the next minute; you know we was belated about starting, and I was scatter-witted. I hope it ain't caused you no great inconvenience ; you ain't wanted it for anything very special, have you ? I s'pose 't was foolish to go f ussin' about the bed, but I thought if you should be sick or anything " —

" Well, I 've got it now," said the deacon, drawing a long breath. " I own I felt some uneasy about it." Presently he went out to the yard, and across the garden, and beyond the garden to the family burying-lot in the field. He would have gone to his parish church to pray if he had been a devout Catholic; as it was, this was the nearest approach he could make to a solemn thanksgiving.

Some of the oldest stones lay flat on the ground, and a network of blackberry vines covered them in part. The leaves were burnt by the sun, and the crickets scrambled among them as the deacon's foot-fall startled them. His first wife and his second wife both were buried there, their resting-places marked by a slate head-stone and a marble one, and it was to this last that the old man went. His first wife had been a plain, hard-worked woman of sterling worth, and his fortunes hucl declined from the day she left him to guard them alone ; but her successor had been a pale and delicate school-teacher, who had roused some unsuspected longing for beauty and romance in Deacon Pi-ice's otherwise prosaic nature. She had seemed like a windflower growing beside a ledge;

and her husband had been forced to confess that she was not fit for a farmer's wife. If he could have had a combination of his two partners, he had once ventured to think, he would have been exactly suited. But it seemed to him, as he stood before the grave with his head bowed, the only way of making some sign of his sorrow, he had wrongfully accused an innocent man, his son and hers; and there he stayed, doing penance as i^-~ best he could, until Eliza's voice called him to the house, and to some sort of comfortable existence and lack of self-reproof.

Before they had finished supper Warren came in, looking flushed and tired ; but he took his seat at the table after a pleasant greeting, and the deacon passed him every plate within reach, treating him with uncommon politeness. The father could not help noticing that his son kept stealing glances at him, and that he looked pleased and satisfied. It seemed to him as if Warren must have known of his suspicions and of their happy ending, but it was discovered presently that the long-toiled-over machine had proved to be a success. Warren had taken it to his former employer at Lowell, who gladly promised, so great was his de-

light with it, to pay the expenses of getting a patent in exchange for a portion of the right. " He said there would be no end to the sale of it," said the young man, looking eagerly at his father's face. "I wouldn't have run off so yesterday, but I was so full of it I could n't bear to think of losing the cars, and I didn't want to say one word about this thing till I was sure.

" I expect I have been slack," he continued with evident effort, while they leaned over the garden fence, and he looked at his father appealingly. " But the fact is, I could n't seem to think of other things ; it took all there was of me to keep right after that. But now I 'm going to take right hold and be some help about the place. I don't seem to want to touch a tool again for a year." Warren looked pale and restless ; the reaction from his long excitement had set in.

The deacon gave a shaky laugh, and struck his son's shoulder by way of a clumsy caress. " Don't you go to frettin' yourself now," he said. " I ain't felt so pleased as I do today since the day you come into the world. I sort of felt certain then that you was goin' to be somebody, I do' know why 't was,"

— and he turned away suddenly toward the house. " If you are as rich as you say you be,

I shouldn't wonder if between us we had n't better get them blinds painted, and smart us up a little, another year. I declare, the old place has begun to look considerable gone to seed."

That night a great thunder-shower broke the spell of the long drought, and afterward, until morning, the rain fell fast upon the thirsty ground. It was a good night to sleep, Eliza said, as she wearily climbed the crooked backstairs at nine o'clock, for there was already a coolness in the air. Eliza never was told the whole of the story about the wallet, for when she heard part of it she only said it was just like a man, — they were generally the most helpless creatur's alive. The deacon might have known she had put it away somewhere. Why did n't he come and ask her ? He never seemed to mistrust that it was a direct p'inting out of his duty to ride over to Somerset to the gathering, and just speak to the folks.

In the early morning, while it was cool and wet, Deacon Price drove up to Captain Stone's farm, and the two selectmen perched

on the chopping-log again, while the confession was made and listened to with great gravity. The captain swore roundly in his satisfaction, and said he was going to have a square talk with Warren, and advise with him a little, for fear that those landsharks down in Lowell should undertake to cheat him. He stowed away the repayment of the loan in one of his big pockets, as if it were of little consequence to him, but he announced with considerable satisfaction at the next selectmen's meeting, that he owned a few planks of that three-masted schooner which the Otises were about ready to launch. And he winked at Deacon Price in a way that their brother Kendall was not able to understand.

MAESH ROSEMARY.

ONE hot afternoon in August, a single moving figure might have been seen following a straight road that crossed the salt marshes of Walpole. Everybody else had either stayed at home or crept into such shade as could be found near at hand. The thermometer marked at least ninety degrees. There was hardly a fishing-boat to be seen on the glistening sea, only far away on the hazy horizon two or three coasting schooners looked like ghostly Flying Dutchmen, becalmed for once and motionless.

Ashore, the flaring light of the sun brought out the fine, clear colors of the level landscape. The marsh grasses were a more vivid green than usual, the brown tops of those that were beginning to go to seed looked almost red, and the soil at the edges of the tide inlets seemed to be melting into

a black, pitchy substance like the dark pigments on a painter's palette. Where the land was higher the hot air flickered above it dizzily. This was not an afternoon that one would naturally choose for a long walk, yet Mr. Jerry Lane stepped briskly forward, and appeared to have more than usual energy. His big boots trod down the soft carpet of pussy-clover that bordered the dusty, whitish road. He struck at the stationary procession of thistles with a little stick as he went by. Flight after flight of yellow butterflies fluttered up as he passed, and then wavered down again to their thistle flowers, while on the shiny cambric back of Jerry's Sunday waistcoat basked at least eight large green-headed flies in complete security.

It was difficult to decide why the Sunday waistcoat should have been put on that Saturday afternoon. Jerry had not thought it important to wear his best boots or best trousers, and had left his coat at home altogether. He smiled as he walked along, and once when he took off his hat, as a light breeze came that way, he waved it triumphantly before he put it on again. Evidently this was no common errand that led him due

west, and made him forget the hot weather, and caused him to shade his eyes with his hand, as he looked eagerly at a clump of trees and the chimney of a small house a lit-tleway beyond the boundary of the marshes, where the higher ground began.

Miss Ann Floyd sat by her favorite window, sewing, twitching her thread less decidedly than usual, and casting a wistful glance now and then down the road, or at the bees in her gay little garden outside. There was a grim expression overshadowing her firmly-set, angular face, and the frown that always appeared on her forehead when she sewed or read the newspaper was deeper and straighter than usual. She did not look as if she were conscious of the heat, though she had dressed herself in an old-fashioned skirt of sprigged lawn and a loose jacket of thin white dimity with out-of-date flowing sleeves. Her sandy hair was smoothly brushed; one lock betrayed a slight crinkle at its edge, but it owed nothing to any encouragement of Nancy Floyd's. A hard, honest, kindly face this was, of a woman whom everybody trusted, who might be expected to give of whatever she had to give,

good measure, pressed down and running over. She was a lonely soul; she had no near relatives in the world. It seemed always as if nature had been mistaken in not planting her somewhere in a large and busy household.

The little square room, kitchen in winter and sitting-room in summer, was as clean and bare and tlu-ifty as one would expect the dwelling-place of such a woman to be. She sat in a straight-backed, splint-bottomed kitchen chair, and always put back her spool with a click on the very same spot on the window-sill. You would think she had done with youth and with love affairs, yet you might as well expect the ancient cherry-tree in the corner of her yard to cease adventuring its white blossoms when the May sun shone! ^o woman in Walpole had more bravely and patiently borne the burden of loneliness and lack of love. Even now her outward behavior gave no hint of the new excitement and delight that filled her heart.

" Land sakes alive! " she says to herself presently, "there comes Jerry Lane. I expect, if he sees me settin' to the winder, he '11 come in an' dawdle round till supper-

time!" But good Nancy Floyd smooths her hair hastily as she rises and drops her work, and steps back toward the middle of the room, watching the gate anxiously all the time. Now, Jerry, with a crestfallen look at the vacant window, makes believe that he is going by, and takes a loitering step or two onward, and then stops short; with a somewhat sheepish smile he leans over the neat picket fence and examines the blue and white and pink larkspur that covers most of the space in the little garden. He takes off his hat again to cool his forehead, and replaces it, without a grand gesture this time, and looks again at the window hopefully. There is a pause. The woman knows that the man is sure she is there; a little blush colors her thin cheeks as she comes boldly to the wide-open front door.

"What do you think of this kind of weather?" asks Jerry Lane complacently, as he leans over the fence, and surrounds himself with an air of self-sacrifice.

" I call it hot," responds the Juliet from her balcony, with deliberate assurance, " but the corn needs sun, everybody says. I should n't have wanted to toil up from the shore under such a glare, if I had been you.

Better come in and set awhih-, and cool off," she added, without any apparent enthusiasm. Jerry was sure to come, anyway. She would rather make the suggestion than have him.

Mr. Lane sauntered in, and seated himself opposite his hostess, beside the other small window, and watched her admiringly as she took up her sewing and worked at it with great spirit and purpose. He clasped his hands together and leaned forward a little. The shaded kitchen was veiy comfortable, after the glaring light outside, and the clean orderliness of the few chairs, and the braided rugs, and the table under the clock, with some larkspur and asparagus in a china vase for decoration, seemed to please him unexpectedly. " Now just see what ways you women folks have of fixing things up smart! " he ventured gallantly.

Nancy's countenance did not forbid further compliment; she looked at the flowers herself, quickly, and explained that she had gathered them a while ago to send to the minister's sister, who kept house for him. " I saw him going by, ami expected he 'd be back this same road. Mis' Elton's be ? n havin' another o' her dyin' spells this noon, and the deacon went by after him hot foot,

I 'd souse her well with stone-cold water. She never sent for me to set up with her; she knows better. Poor man, 't was likely he was right into the middle of to-morrow's sermon. 'T ain't considerate of the deacon, and when he knows he's got a fool for a wife, he need n't go round persuading other folks she's so suffering as she makes out. They ain't got no larkspur this year to the parsonage, and I was going to let the minister take this over to Amandy; but I see his wagon over on the other road, going towards the village, about an hour after he went by here."

It seemed to be a relief to tell somebody all these things after such a season of forced repression, and Jerry listened with gratifying interest. " How you do see through folks ! " he exclaimed in a mild voice. Jerry could be very soft spoken if he thought best. " Mis' Elton's a die-away lookin' creatur'. I heard of her saying last Sunday, comin' out o' meetin', that she made an effort to git there once more, but she expected 'twould be the last time. Looks as if she eat well, don't she?" he concluded in a meditative tone.

" Eat! " exclaimed the hostess, with snap-ping eyes. " There ain't no woman in town, sick or well, can lay aside the food that she does. 'T ain't to the table afore folks, but she goes seeking round in the cupboards half a dozen times a day. An' I 've heard her remark 't was the last time she ever expected to visit the sanctuary as much as a dozen times within five years."

" Some places I 've sailed to they 'd have hit her over the head with a club long ago," said Jerry, with an utter lack of sympathy that was startling. " Well, I must be get-tin' back again. Talkin' of eatin' makes us think o' supper-time. Must be past five, ain't it ? I thought I 'd just step up to see if there wa'n't anything I could lend a hand about, this hot day."

Sensible Ann Floyd folded her hands over her sewing, as it lay in her lap, and looked straight before her without seeing the pleading face of the guest. This moment was a great crisis in her life. She was conscious of it, and knew well enough that upon her next words would depend the course of future events. The man who waited to hear what she had to say was indeed many years younger than she, was shiftless and vacillating. He had drifted to Walpole from no-body knew where, and possessed many qualities which she had openly rebuked and despised in other men. True enough, he was good-looking, but that did not atone for the lacks of his character and reputation. Yet she knew herself to be the better man of the two, and since she had surmounted many obstacles already she was confident that, with a push here and a pull there to steady him, she could keep him in good trim. The winters were so long and lonely; her life was in many ways hungry and desolate in spite of its thrift and conformity. She had laughed scornfully when he stopped, one day in the spring, and offered to help her weed her garden ; she had even joked with one of the neighbors about it. Jerry had been growing more and more friendly and pleasant ever since. His ease-loving, careless nature was like a comfortable cushion for hers, with its angles, its melancholy anticipations and self-questionings. But Jerry liked her, and if she liked him and married him, and took him home, it was nobody's business , and in that moment of surrender to Jerry's cause she arrayed herself at his right hand against the rest of the world, ready for warfare with any and all of its opinions.

She was suddenly aware of the sunburnt face and light, curling hair of her undeclared lover, at the other end of the painted table with its folded leaf. She smiled at him vacantly across the larkspur; then she gave a little start, and was afraid that her thoughts had wandered longer than was seemly. The kitchen clock was ticking faster than usual, as if it were trying to attract attention.

" I guess I '11 be getting home," repeated the visitor ruefully, and rose from his chair, but hesitated again at an unfamiliar expression upon his companion's face.

" I don't know as I 've got anything extra for supper, but you stop," she said, "an* take what there is. I would n't go back across them marshes right in this heat."

Jerry Lane had a lively sense of humor, and a queer feeling of merriment stole over him now, as he watched the mistress of the house. She had risen, too ; she looked so simple and so frankly sentimental, there was such an incongruous coyness added to her ^usually straightforward, angular appearance, that his instinctive laughter nearly got the better of him, and might have lost him the •prize for which he had been waiting these

many months. But Jerry behaved like a man: he stepped forward and kissed Ann Floyd ; he held her fast with one arm as he stood beside her, and kissed her again and again. She was a dear good woman. She had a fresh young heart, in spite of the straight wrinkle in her forehead and her work-worn hands. She had wanted all her days for this joy of having a lover.

II.

EVEN Mrs. Elton revived for a day or two under the tonic of such a piece of news. That was what Jerry Lane had hung round for all summer, everybody knew at last. Now he would strike work and live at his ease, the men grumbled to each other ; but all the women of Walpole deplored most the weakness and foolishness of the elderly bride. Ann Floyd was comfortably off, and had something laid by for a rainy day ; she would have done vastly better to deny herself such an expensive and utterly worthless luxury as the kind of husband Jerry Lane would make. He had idled away his life. He earned a little money now and then in

seafaring pursuits, but was too lazy, in the shore parlance, to tend lobster-pots. What was energetic Ann Floyd going to do with him ? She was always at work, always equal I to emergencies, and entirely opposed to \dullness and idleness and even placidity, ohe often avowed scornfully that she liked people who-had some snap to them, and now she had chosen for a husband the laziest man in Walpole. " Dear sakes," one woman said to another, as they heard the news, " there 's no fool like an old fool! "

The days went quickly by, while Miss Ann made her plain wedding clothes. If people expected her to put on airs of youth they were disappointed. Her wedding bonnet was the same sort of bonnet she had worn for a dozen years, and one disappointed critic deplored the fact that she had spruced up so little, and kept on dressing old enough to look like Jerry Lane's mother. As her acquaintances met her they looked at her with close scrutiny, expecting to see some outward trace of such a silly, um-liar-acteristic departure from good sense and discretion. But Miss Floyd, while she was still Miss Floyd, displayed no silliness and behaved with dignity, while on the Sunday

after a quiet marriage at the parsonage she and Jerry Lane walked up the side aisle together to their pew, the picture of middle-aged sobriety and respectability. Their fellow-parishioners, having recovered from their first astonishment and amusement, settled down to the belief that the newly married pair understood their own business best, and that if anybody could make the best of Jerry and get any work out of him, it was his capable wife.

" And if she undertakes to drive him too hard he can slip off to sea, and they '11 be rid of each other," commented one of Jerry's 'longshore companions, as if it were only reasonable that some refuge should be afforded to those who make mistakes in matrimony.

There did not seem to be any mistake at first, or for a good many months afterward. The husband liked the comfort that came from such good housekeeping, and enjoyed a deep sense of having made a good anchorage in a well-sheltered harbor, after many years of thriftless improvidence and drifting to and fro. There were some hindrances to perfect happiness: he had to forego long

seasons of gossip with his particular friend-;. and the outdoor work which was expected of him, though by no means heavy for a person of his strength, fettered his freedom not a little. To chop wood, and take care of a cow, and bring a pail of water now and then, did not weary him so much as it made him practically understand the truth of weakly Sister Elton's remark, that life was a constant chore. And when poor Jerry, for lack of other interest, fancied that his health was giving way mysteriously, and brought home a bottle of strong liquor to be used in case of sickness, and placed it conveniently in the shed, Mrs. Lane locked it up in the small chimney cupboard where she kept her camphor bottle and her opodeldoc and the other family medicines. She was not harsh with her husband. She cherished him tenderly, and worked diligently at her trade of tailoress, singing her hymns gayly in summer weather ; for she never had been so happy as now, when there was somebody to please beside herself, to cook for and sew for, and to live with and love. But Jerry complained more and more in his inmost heart that his wife expected too much of him. Presently he resumed an old habit of

resorting to the least respected of the two country stores of that neighborhood, and sat in the row of loafers on the outer steps. " Sakes alive," said a shrewd observer one day, " the fools set there and talk and talk about what they went through when they follered the sea, and when the women-folks comes tradin' they are obleeged to climb right over 'em."

Things grew worse and worse, until one day Jerry Lane came home a little late to dinner, and found his wife unusually grim-faced and impatient. He took his seat with an amiable smile, and showed in every way a fine determination not to lose his temper because somebody else had. It was one of the days when he looked almost boyish and entirely irresponsible. His hair was bright and curly from the dampness of the east wind, and his wife was forced to remember how, in the days of their courtship, she used to wish that she could pull one of the curling locks straight, for the pleasure of seeing it fly back. Nancy felt old and tired, and was hurt in her very soul by the contrast between herself and her husband. " No wonder I am aging, having to lug everything on my shoulders," she thought. Jerry had

forgotten to do whatever she had asked him for a day or two. He had started out that morning to go lobstering, but returned from the direction of the village.

" Nancy," he said pleasantly, after he had begun his dinner, a silent and solitary meal, while his wife stitched busily by the window, and refused to look at him, — " Nancy, I've been thinking a good deal about a project."

"I hope it ain't going to cost so much and bring in so little as your other notions have, then," she responded quickly; though somehow a memory of the hot day when Jerry came and stood outside the fence, and kissed her when it was settled he should stay to supper, — a memory of that day would keep fading and brightening in her mind.

" Yes," said Jerry humbly, " I ain't done right, Nancy. I ain't done my part for our livin'. I 've let it sag right on to you, most ever since we was married. There was that spell when I was kind of weakly, and had a pain acrost me. I tell you what it is: I never was good for nothin' ashore, but now I 've got my strength up I 'm going to show ye what I can do. I 'm promised to

ship with Cap'n Low's brother, Skipper Nathan, that sails out o' Eastport in the coasting
trade, lumber and so on. I shall get good wage's, and you shall keep the whole on 't 'cept what I need for clothes."

" You need n't be so plaintive," said Ann in a sharp voice. " You can go if you want to. I have always been able to take care of myself, but when it comes to maintainin' two, 't ain't so easy. When be you goin' ? "

"I expected you would be distressed," mourned Jerry, his face falling at this outbreak. " Nancy, you need n't be so quick. 'T ain't as if I had n't always set consid'able by ye, if I be wuthless."

Nancy's eyes flashed fire as she turned hastily away. Hardly knowing where she went, she passed through the open doorway, and crossed the clean green turf of the narrow side yard, and leaned over the garden fence. The young cabbages and cucumbers were nearly buried in weeds, and the currant bushes were fast being turned into skeletons by the ravaging worms. Jerry had forgotten to sprinkle them with hellebore, after all, though she had put the watering-pot into his very hand the evening before. She did not like to have the whole town laugh at her for hiring a man to do his work; she was busy from early morning
until late night, but she could not do everything herself. She had been a fool to marry this man, she told herself at last, and a sul-len discontent and rage, that had been of slow but certain growth, made her long to free herself from this unprofitable hindrance for a time, at any rate. Go to sea ? Yes, that was the best thing that could happen. Perhaps when he had worked hard a while on schooner fare, he would come home and be good for something!

Jerry finished his dinner in the course of time, and then sought his wife. It was not like her to go away in this silent fashion. Of late her gift of speech had been proved sufficiently formidable, and yet she had never looked so resolutely angry as to-day.

" Nancy," he began, — " Nancy, girl! I ain't goin' off to leave you, if your heart's set against it. I '11 spudge up and take right holt."

But the wife turned slowly from the fence and faced him. Her eyes looked as if she had been crying. " You need n't stay on my account," she said. " I '11 go right to work an' fit ye out. I 'm sick of your meechin' talk, and I don't want to hear no more of it. Ef / was a man " —

Jerry Lane looked crestfallen for a minute or two; but when his stern partner in life had disappeared within the house, he slunk away among the apple-trees of the little orchard, and sat down on the grass in a shady spot. It was getting to be warm weather, but he would go round and hoe the old girl's garden stuff by and by. There would be something going on aboard the schooner, and with delicious anticipation of future pleasure the delinquent Jerry struck his knee with his hand, as if he were clapping a crony on the shoulder. He also winked several times at the same fancied companion. Then, with a comfortable chuckle, he laid himself down, and pulled his old hat over his eyes, and went to sleep, while the weeds grew at their own sweet will, and the currant worms went looping and devouring from twig to twig.

SUMMER went by, and winter began, and Mr. Jerry Lane did not reappear. He had promised to return in September when he parted from his wife early in June, for
Nancy had relented a little at the last, and sorrowed at the prospect of so long a separation. She had already learned the vacillations and uncertainties of her husband's character; but though she accepted the truth that her marriage had been in every way a piece of foolishness, she still clung affectionately to his assumed fondness for her. She could not believe that this marriage was only one of his makeshifts, and that as soon as he grew tired of the constraint he would be ready to throw the benefits of respectable home life to the four winds. A little

sentimental speech-making and a few kisses the morning he went away, and the gratitude he might well have shown for her generous care-taking and provision for his voyage won her soft heart back again, and made poor, elderly, simple-hearted Nancy watch him cross the marshes with tears and foreboding. If she could have called him back that day, she would have done so and been thankful. And all summer and winter, whenever the wind blew and thrashed the drooping elm boughs against the low roof over her head, she was as full of fears and anxieties as if Jerry were her only son and making his first voyage at sea. The neigh-

bors pitied her for her disappointment. They liked Nancy ; but they could not help saying, " I told you so." It would have been impossible not to respect the brave way in which she met the world's eye, and carried herself with innocent unconsciousness of having committed so laughable and unrewarding a folly. The loafers on the store steps had been unwontedly diverted one day, when Jerry, who was their chief wit and spokesman, rose slowly from his place, and said in pious tones, " Boys, I must go this minute. Grandma will keep dinner waiting." Mrs. Ann Lane did not show in her aging face how young her heart was, and after the schooner Susan Barnes had departed she seemed to pass swiftly from middle life and an almost youthful vigor to early age and a look of spent strength and dissatisfaction. " I suppose he did find it stupid," she assured herself, with wistful yearning for his rough words of praise, when she sat down alone to her dinner, or looked up sadly from her work, and missed the amusing though unedifying conversation he was wont to offer on stormy winter nights. How many of his marvelous tales were true she never cared to ask. He had

come and gone, and she forgave him his shortcomings, and longed for his society with a heavy heart.

One spring day there was news in the Boston paper of the loss of the schooner Susan Barnes with all on board, and Nancy Lane's best friends shook their sage heads, and declared that as far as regarded that idle vagabond, Jerry Lane, it was all for the best. Nobody was interested in any other member of the crew, so the misfortune of the Susan Barnes seemed of but slight consequence in Walpole, she having passed out of her former owners' hands the autumn before. Jerry had stuck by the ship ; at least, so he had sent word then to his wife by Skipper Nathan Low. The Susan Barnes was to sail regularly between Shediac and Newfoundland, and Jerry sent five dollars to Nancy, and promised to pay her a visit soon. " Tell her I 'm layin' up somethin' handsome," he told the skipper with a grin, " and I 've got some folks in Newfoundland I '11 visit with on this voyage, and then I '11 come ashore for good and farm it."

Mrs. Lane took the five dollars from the skipper as proudly as if Jerry had done the same thing so many times before that she

hardly noticed it. The skipper gave the messages from Jerry, and felt that he had done the proper thing. When the news came long afterward that the schooner was lost, that was the next thing that Nancy knew about her wandering mate ; and after the minister had come solemnly to inform her of her bereavement, and had gone away again, and she sat down and looked her widowhood in the face, there was not a sadder nor a lonelier woman in the town of Walpole.

All the neighbors came to condole with our heroine, and, though nobody was aware of it, from that time she was really happier and better satisfied with life than she had ever been before. Now that she had an ideal Jerry Lane to mourn over and think about, to cherish and admire, she was day by day slowly forgetting the trouble he had been and the bitter shame of him, and exalting his memory to something near saint-liness. "He meant well," she told herself again and again. She thought nobody could tell so good a story ; she felt that with her own bustling, capable ways he had no chance to do much that he might have done. She had been too quick with him, and alas, alas I

how much better she would know how to treat him if she could only see him again! A sense of relief at his absence made her continually assure herself of her great loss, and, false even to herself, she mourned her sometime lover diligently, and tried to think herself a broken-hearted woman. It was thought among those who knew Nancy Lane best that she would recover her spirits in time, but Jerry's wildest anticipations of a proper respect to his memory were more than realized in the first two years after the schooner Susan Barnes went to the bottom of the sea. /His wife mourned for the man he ought to have been, not for the real Jerry, but she had loved him enough in the beginning to make her own love a precious possession for all time to come. It did not matter much, after all, what manner of man he was ; she had found in him something on which to spend her hoarded affection.

IV.

NANCY LANE was a peaceable woman and a good neighbor, but she never had been able to get on with one fellow townswornan,

and that was Mrs. Deacon Elton. They managed to keep each other provoked and teased from one year's end to the other, and each good soul felt herself under a moral microscope, and understood that she was judged by a not very lenient criticism and discussion. Mrs. Lane clad herself in simple black after the news came of her husband's timely death, and Mrs. Elton made one of her farewell pilgrimages to church to see the new-made widow walk up the aisle.

" She need n't tell me she lays that affliction so much to heart," the deacon's wife sniffed faintly, after her exhaustion had been met by proper treatment of camphor and a glass of currant wine, at the parsonage, where she rested a while after service. " Nancy Floyd knows she's well through with such a piece of nonsense. If I had had my health, I should have spoken with her and urged her not to take the step in the first place. She has n't spoken six beholden words to me since that vagabond come to Walpole. I dare say she may have heard something I said at the time she married. I declare for 't, I never was so outdone as when the deacon came home and informed me Nancy Floyd was going to be married.

She let herself down too low to ever hold the place again that she used to hold in folks' minds. And it's my opinion," said the sharp-eyed little woman, " she ain't got through with her pay yet."

But Mrs. Elton did not half comprehend the unconscious prophecy with which her words were freighted.

The months passed by : summer and winter came and went, and even those few persons who were misled by Nancy Lane's stern visage and forbidding exterior into forgetting her kind heart were at last won over to friendliness by her renewed devotion to the sick and old people of the rural community. She was so tender to little children that they all loved her dearly. She was ready to go to any household that needed help, and in spite of her ceaseless industry with her needle she found many a chance to do good, and help her neighbors to lift and carry the burdens of their lives. She blossomed out suddenly into a lovely, painstaking eagerness to be of use; it seemed as if her affectionate heart, once made generous, must go on spending its wealth wherever it could find an excuse. Even Mrs. Elton her-

self was touched by her old enemy's evident wish to be friends, and said nothing more about poor Nancy's looking as savage as a hawk. The only thing to admit was the truth that her affliction had proved a blessing to her.. And it was in a truly kind and compassionate spirit that, after hearing a shocking piece of news, the deacon's hysterical wife forbore to spread it far and wide through the town first, and went down to the Widow Lane's one September afternoon.

Nancy was stitching busily upon the deacon's new coat, and looked up with a friendly smile as her guest came in, in spite of an instinctive shrug as she had seen her coming up the yard. The dislike of the poor souls for each other was deeper than their philosophy could reach.

Mrs. Elton spent some minutes in the unnecessary endeavor to regain her breath, and to her surprise found she must make a real effort before she could tell her unwelcome news. She had been so full of it all the way from home that she had rehearsed the whole interview; now she hardly knew how to begin. Nancy looked serener than usual, but there was something wistful about her face as she glanced across the room,

presently, as if to understand the reason of the long pause. The clock ticked loudly; the kitten clattered a spool against the table-leg, and had begun to snarl the thread round her busy paws, and Nancy looked down and saw her; then the instant consciousness of there being some unhappy reason for Mrs. Elton's call made her forget the creature's mischief, and anxiously lay down her work to listen.

" Capt'in Nathan Low was to our house to dinner," the guest began. " He 's bargaining with the deacon about some hay. He's got a new schooner, Capt'in Nathan has, and is going to build up a regular business of freighting hay to Boston by sea. There's no market to speak of about here, unless you haul it way over to Downer, and you can't make but one turn a day."

" 'T would be a good thing," replied Nancy, trying to think that this was all, and perhaps the deacon wanted to hire her own field another year. He had underpaid her once, and they had not been on particularly good terms ever since. She would make her own bargains with Skipper Low, she thanked him and his wife !

" He 's been down to the provinces these
two or three years back, you know," the whining voice went on, and straightforward Ann Lane felt the old animosity rising within her. " At dinner-time I wa'n't able to eat much of anything, and so I was talking with Capt'in Nathan, and asking him some questions about them parts; and I expressed something about the mercy 't was his life should ha' been spared when that schooner, the Susan Barnes, was lost so quick after he sold out his part of her. And I put in a word, bein' 's we were neighbors, about how edifyin' your course had be'n under affliction. I noticed then he 'd looked sort o' queer whilst I was talkin', but there was all the folks to the table, and you know he 's a very cautious man, so he spoke of somethin' else. 'T wa'n't half an hour after dinner, I was comin' in with some plates and cups, tryin' to help what my stren'th would let me, and says he, ' Step out a little ways into the piece with me, Mis' Elton. I want to have a word with ye.' I went, too, spite o' my neuralgy, for I saw he 'd got somethin' on his mind. * Look here,' says he, ' I gathered from the way you spoke that Jerry Lane's wife expects he 's dead.' Certain, says I, his name was in the list o' the
Susan Barnes's crew, and we read it in the paper. * No,' says he to me, ' he ran away the day they sailed ; he wa'ii't aboard, and he's livin' with another woman down to Shediac.' Them was his very words."

Nancy Lane sank back in her chair, and covered her horror-stricken eyes with her hands. " 'T ain't pleasant news to have to tell," Sister Elton went on mildly, yet with evident relish and full command of the occasion. " He said he seen Jerry the morning he came away. I thought you ought to know it. I '11 tell you one thing, Nancy : I told the skipper to keep still about it, and now I 've told you, I won't spread it no further to set folks a-talking. I '11 keep it secret till you say the word. There ain't much trafficking betwixt here and there, and he 's dead to you, certain, as much as if he laid up here in the burying-ground."

Nancy had bowed her head upon the table ; the thin sandy hair was streaked with gray. She did not answer one word; this was the hardest blow of all.

" I 'm much obliged to you for being so friendly," she said after a few minutes, looking straight before her now in a dazed sort of way, and lifting the new coat from the
floor, where it had fallen. " Yes, he 's dead to me, — worse than dead, a good deal," and her lip quivered. " I can't seem to bring my thoughts to bear. I 've got so used to thinkin' — No, don't you say nothin' to the folks yet. I 'd do as much for you." And Mrs. Elton knew that the smitten fellow-creature before her spoke the truth, and forebore.

Two or three days came and went, and with every hour the quiet, simple-hearted woman felt more grieved and unsteady in mind and body. Such a shattering thunderbolt of news rarely falls into a human life. She could" not sleep; she wandered to and fro in the little house, and cried until she could cry no longer. Then a great rage spurred and excited her. She would go to Shediac, and call Jerry Lane to account. She would accuse him face to face ; and the woman whom he was deceiving, as perhaps he had deceived her, should know the baseness and cowardice of this miserable man. So, dressed in her respectable Sunday clothes, in the gray bonnet and shawl that never had known any journeys except to meeting, or to a country funeral or quiet
holiday-making, Nancy Lane trusted herself for the first time to the bewildering railway, to the temptations and dangers of the wide world outside the bounds of Walpole.

Two or three aays later still, the quaint, thin figure familiar in Walpole highways flitted down the street of a provincial town. In the most primitive region of China this woman could hardly have felt a greater sense of foreign life and strangeness. At another time her native good sense and shrewd observation would have delighted in the experiences of this first week of travel, but she was too sternly angry and aggrieved, too deeply plunged in a survey of her own calamity, to take much notice of what was going on about her. Later she condemned the unworthy folly of the whole errand, but in these days the impulse to seek the culprit and confront him was irresistible.

The innkeeper's wife, a kindly creature, urged this puzzling guest to wait and rest and eat some supper, but Nancy refused, and without asking her way left the brightly lighted, flaring little public room, where curious eyes already offended her, and went out into the damp twilight. The voices of the street boys sounded outlandish, and she

felt more and more lonely. She longed for Jerry to appear for protection's sake : she forgot why she sought him, and was eager to shelter herself behind the flimsy bulwark of his manhood. She rebuked herself presently with terrible bitterness for a womanish wonder whether he would say, " Why, Nancy, girl! " and be glad to see her. Poor woman, it was a work-laden, serious girlhood that had been hers, at any rate. The power of giving her whole self in unselfish, enthusiastic, patient devotion had not belonged to her youth only; it had sprung fresh and blossoming in her heart as every new year came and went.

One might have seen her stealing through the shadows, skirting the edge of a lumberyard, stepping among the refuse of the harbor side, asking a question timidly now and then of some passer-by. Yes, they knew Jerry Lane, — his house was only a little way off ; and one curious and compassionate Scotchman, divining by some inner sense the exciting nature of the errand, turned back, and offered fruitlessly to go with the stranger. " You know the man ? " he asked. "He is his own enemy, but doing better now that he is married. He minds his work,

I know that well; and he's taken a good wife." Nancy's heart beat faster with honest pride for a moment, until the shadow of the ugly truth and reality made it sink back to heaviness, and the fire of her smouldering rage was again kindled. She would speak to Jerry face to face before she slept, and a horrible contempt and scorn were ready for him, as with a glance either way along the road she entered the narrow yard, and went noiselessly toward the window of a low, poor-looking house, from whence a bright light was shining out into the night.

Yes, there was Jerry, and it seemed as if she must faint and fall at the sight of him. How young he looked still! The thought smote her like a blow. They never were mates for each other, Jerry and she. Her own life was waning; she was an old woman.

He never had been so thrifty and respectable before ; the other woman ought to know the savage truth about him, for all that! But at that moment the other woman stooped beside the supper table, and lifted a baby from its cradle, and put the dear, live little thing into its father's arms. The baby was wide-awake, and laughed at Jerry, who laughed back again, and it reached up

to catch at a handful of the curly hair which had been poor Nancy's delight.

The other woman stood there looking at them, full of pride and love. She was young, and trig, and neat. She looked a brisk, efficient little creature. Perhaps Jerry would make something of himself now; he always had it in him. The tears were running down Nancy's cheeks; the rain, too, had begun to fall. She stood there watching the little household sit down to supper, and noticed with eager envy how well cooked the food was, and how hungrily the master of the house ate what was put before him. All thoughts of ending the new wife's sin and folly vanished away. She could not enter in and break another heart ; hers was broken already, and it would not matter. And Nancy Lane, a widow indeed, crept away again, as silently as she had come, to c think what was best to be done, to find alternate woe and comfort in the memory of the sight she had seen.

The little house at the edge of the Wai-pole marshes seemed full of blessed shelter and comfort the evening that its forsaken mistress came back to it Her strength was spent; she felt much more desolate now that she had seen with her own eyes that Jerry Lane was alive than when she had counted him among the dead. An uncharacteristic disregard of the laws of the land filled this good woman's mind. Jerry had his life to live, and she wished him no harm. She wondei-ed often how the baby grew, and fancied again and again the changes and conditions of the far-away household. Alas! she knew only too well the weakness of the man, and once she exclaimed, in a grim outburst of impatience, " I 'd rather others should have to cope with him than me!"

But that evening, when she came back from Shediac, and sat in the dark for a long time, lest Mrs. Elton should see the light and risk her life in the evening air to bring unwelcome sympathy, — that evening, I say, came the hardest moment of all, when Ann Floyd, tailoress, of so many virtuous, self-respecting years, whose idol had turned to clay, who was shamed, disgraced, and wronged, sat down alone to supper in the little kitchen.

She had put one cup and saucer on the table and then stood and looked at them through bitter tears. Somehow a conscious-

ness of her solitary age, her uncompanioned future, rushed through her mind; the failure of her best earthly hope was enough to break a stronger woman's heart.

Who can laugh at my Marsh Rosemary, or who can cry, for that matter ? The gray primness of the plant is made up from a hundred colors if you look close enough to find them. This Marsh Rosemary stands in her own place, and holds her dry leaves and tiny blossoms steadily toward the same sun that the pink lotus blooms for, and the white rose.

A WHITE HERON.

THE woods were already filled with shadows one June evening, just before eight o'clock, though a bright sunset still glimmered faintly among the trunks of the trees. A little girl was driving home her cow, a plodding, dilatory, provoking creature in her behavior, but a valued companion for all that. They were going away from the western light, and striking deep into the dark woods, but their feet were familiar with the path, and it was no matter whether their eyes could see it or not.

There was hardly a night the summer through when the old cow could be found waiting at the pasture bars; on the contrary, it was her greatest pleasure to hide herself away among the high huckleberry bushes, and though she wore a loud bell she had made the discovery that if one stood per-

fectly still it would not ring. So Sylvia had to hunt for her until she found her, and call Co' ! Co'! with never an answering Moo, until her childish patience was quite spent. If the creature had not given good milk and plenty of it, the case would have seemed very different to her owners. Besides, Sylvia had all the time there was, and very little use to make of it. Sometimes in pleasant weather it was a consolation to look upon the cow's pranks as an intelligent attempt to play hide and seek, and as the child had no playmates she lent herself to this amusement with a good deal of zest. Though this chase had been so long that the wary animal herself had given an unusual signal of her whereabouts, Sylvia had only laughed when she came upon Mistress Moolly at the swamp-side, and urged her affectionately homeward with a twig of birch leaves. The old cow was not inclined to wander farther, she even turned in the right direction for once as they left the pasture, and stepped along the road at a good pace. She was quite ready to be milked now, and seldom stopped to browse. Sylvia wondered what her

grandmother would say because they were so late. It was a great while since she
        had left home at half past five o'clock, but everybody knew the difficulty of making this cnaiul a short one. Mrs. Tilley had chased the horned torment too many summer evenings herself to blame any one else for lingering, and was only thankful as she waited that she had Sylvia, nowadays, to give such valuable assistance. The good woman suspected that Sylvia loitered occasionally on her own account; there never was such a child for straying about out-of-doors since the world was made! Everybody said that it was a good change for a little maid who had tried to grow for eight years in a crowded manufacturing town, but, as for Sylvia herself, it seemed as if she never had been alive at all before she came to live at the farm. She thought often with wistful compassion of a wretched diy geranium that belonged to a town neighbor.
        "' Afraid of folks,' " old Mrs. Tilley said to herself, with a smile, after she had made the unlikely choice of Sylvia from her daughter's houseful of children, and was returning to the farm. "' Afraid of folks,' they said! I guess she won't be troubled no great with 'em up to the old place!" When they reached the door of the lonely
        house and stopped to unlock it, and the cat came to purr loudly, and rub against them, a deserted pussy, indeed, but fat with young robins, Sylvia whispered that this was a beautiful place to live in, and she never should wish to go home.
        The companions followed the shady wood-road, the cow taking slow steps, and the child very fast ones. The cow stopped long at the brook to drink, as if the pasture were not half a swamp, and Sylvia stood still and waited, letting her bare feet cool themselves in the shoal water, while the great twilight moths struck softly against her. She waded on through the brook as the cow moved away, and listened to the thrushes with a heart that beat fast with pleasure. There was a stirring in the great boughs overhead. They were full of little birds and beasts that seemed to be wide-awake, and going about their world, or else saying good-night to each other in sleepy twitters. Sylvia herself felt sleepy as she walked along. However, it was not much farther to the house, and the air was soft and sweet. She was not often in the woods so late as this, and it made her feel as if she were a part of the
        gray shadows and the moving leaves. She was just thinking how long it seemed since she first came to the farm a year ago, and wondering if everything went on in the noisy town just the same as when she was there; the thought of the great red - faced boy who used to chase and frighten her made her hurry along the path to escape from the shadow of the trees.
        Suddenly this little woods-girl is horror-stricken to hear a clear whistle not very far away. Not a bird's whistle, which would have a sort of friendliness, but a boy's whistle, determined, and somewhat aggressive. Sylvia left the cow to whatever sad fate might await her, and stepped discreetly aside into the bushes, but she was just too late. The enemy had discovered her, and called out in a very cheerful and persuasive tone, "Halloa, little girl, how far is it to the road ? " and trembling Sylvia answered almost inaudibly, " A good ways."
        She did not dare to look boldly at the tall young man, who carried a gun over his shoulder, but she came out of her bush and again followed the cow, while he walked alongside.
        "I have been hunting for some birds,"
        the stranger said kindly, " and I have lost my way, and need a friend very much. Don't be afraid," he added gallantly. "Speak up and tell me what your name is, and whether you think I can spend the night at your house, and go out gunning e^rly in the morning."
        Sylvia was more alarmed than before. Would not her grandmother consider her much to blame ? But who could have foreseen such an accident as this ? It did not appear to be her fault, and she hung her head as if the stem of it were broken, but managed to answer " Sylvy," with

much effort when her companion again asked her name.

Mrs. Tilley was standing in the doorway when the trio came into view. The cow gave a loud inoo by way of explanation.

" Yes, you'd better speak up for yourself, you old trial! Where 'd she tucked herself away this time, Sylvy?" Sylvia kept an awed silence ; she knew by instinct that her grandmother did not comprehend the gravity of the situation. She must be mistaking the stranger for one of the farmer-lads of the region.

The young man stood his gun beside the door, and dropped a heavy game-bag beside it; then he bade Mrs. Tilley good-evening, and repeated his wayfarer's story, and asked if he could have a night's lodging.

" Put me anywhere you like," he said. " I must be off early in the morning, before day; but I am very hungry, indeed. You can give me some milk at any rate, that's plain."

" Dear sakes, yes," responded the hostess, whose long slumbering hospitality seemed to be easily awakened. " You might fare better if you went out on the main road a mile or so, but you 're welcome to what we 've got. I '11 milk right off, and you make yourself at home. You can sleep on husks or feathers," she proffered graciously. " I raised them all myself. There's good pasturing for geese just below here towards the ma'sh. Now step round and set a plate for the gentleman, Sylvy!" And Sylvia promptly stepped. She was glad to have something to do, and she was hungry herself.

It was a surprise to find so clean and comfortable a little dwelling in this New England wilderness. The young man had known the horrors of its most primitive housekeeping, and the dreary squalor of that level of

society which does not rebel at the companionship of hens. This was the best thrift of an old-fashioned farmstead, though on such a small scale that it seemed like a hermitage. He listened eagerly to the old woman's quaint talk, he watched Sylvia's pale face and shining gray eyes with ever growing enthusiasm, and insisted that this was the best supper he had eaten for a month; then, afterward, the new - made friends sat down in the doorway together while the moon came up.

Soon it would be berry-time, and Sylvia was a great help at picking. The cow was a good milker, though a plaguy thing to keep track of, the hostess gossiped frankly, adding presently that she had buried four children, so that Sylvia's mother, and a son (who might be dead) in California were all the children she had left. "Dan, my boy, was a great hand to go gunning," she explained sadly. " I never wanted for pa'tridges or gray squer'ls while he was to home. He 's been a great wand'rer, I expect, and he's no hand to write letters. There, I don't blame him, I 'd ha' seen the world myself if it had been so I could.

"Sylvia takes after him," the grand-

mother continued affectionately, after a minute's pause. "There ain't a foot o' ground she don't know her way over, and the wild creatur's counts her one o' themselves. Squer'ls she '11 tame to come an' feed right out o' her hands, and all sorts o' birds. Last winter she got the jay-birds to bangeing here, and I believe she 'd 'a' scanted herself of her own meals to have plenty to throw out amongst 'em, if I had n't kep' watch. Anything but crows, I tell her, I 'm willin' to help suppo»t, — though Dan he went an' tamed one o' them that did seem to have reason same as folks. It was round here a good spell after he went away. Dan an' his father they did n't hitch, — but he never held up his head ag'in after Dan had dared him an' gone off."

The guest did not notice this hint of family sorrows in his eager interest in something else.

" So Sylvy knows all about birds, does she ? " he exclaimed, as he looked round at the little girl who sat, very demure but increasingly sleepy, in the moonlight. " I am making a collection of birds myself. I have been at it ever since I was a boy." (Mrs. Tilley smiled.) " There are two or three

very rare ones I have been hunting for these five years. I mean to get them on my own ground if they can be found."

" Do you cage 'em up ? " asked Mrs. Til-ley doubtfully, in response to this enthusiastic announcement.

" Oh, no, they 're stuffed and preserved, dozens and dozens of them," said the ornithologist, " and I have shot or snared every one myself. I caught a glimpse of a white heron three miles from here on Saturday, and I have followed it in this direction. They have never been found in this district at all. The little white heron, it is," and he turned again to look at Sylvia with the hope of discovering that the rare bird was one of her acquaintants.

But Sylvia was watching a hop-toad in the narrow footpath.

" You would know the heron if you saw it," the stranger continued eagerly. " A queer tall white bird with soft feathers and long thin legs. And it would have a nest perhaps in the top of a high tree, made of sticks, something like a hawk's nest."

Sylvia's heart gave a wild beat ; she knew that strange white bird, and had once stolen softly near where it stood in some bright

green swamp grass, away over at the other side of the woods. There was an open place where the sunshine always seemed strangely yellow and hot, where tall, nodding rushes grew, and her grandmother had warned her that she might sink in the soft black mud underneath and never be heard of more. Not far beyond were the salt marshes and beyond those was the sea, the sea which Sylvia wondered and dreamed about, but never had looked upon, though its great voice could often be heard above the noise of the woods on stormy nights.

" I can't think of anything I should like so much as to find that heron's nest," the handsome stranger was saying. " I would give ten dollars to anybody who could show it to me," he added desperately, " and I mean to spend my whole vacation hunting for it if need be. Perhaps it was only migrating, or had been chased out of its own region by some bird of prey."

Mrs. Tilley gave amazed attention to all this, but Sylvia still watched the toad, not divining, as she might have done at some calmer time, that the creature wished to get to its hole under the doorstep, and was much hindered by the unusual spectators at

that hour of the evening. No amount of thought, that night, could decide how many wished-for treasures the ten dollars, so lightly spoken of, would buy.

The next day the young sportsman hovered about the woods, and Sylvia kept him company, having lost her first fear of the friendly lad, who proved to be most kind and sympathetic. He told her many things about the birds and what they knew and where they lived and what they did with themselves. And he gave her a jack-knife, which she thought as great a treasure as if she were a desert-islander. All day long he did not once make her troubled or afraid except when he brought down some unsuspecting singing creature from its bough. Sylvia would have liked him vastly better without his gun ; she could not understand why he killed the very birds he seemed to like so much. But as the day waned, Sylvia still watched the young man with loving admiration. She had never seen anybody so charming and delightful; the woman's heart, asleep in the child, was vaguely thrilled by a dream of love. Some premonition of that great power stirred and swayed these young

foresters who traversed the solemn woodlands with soft-footed silent care. They stopped to listen to a bird's song; they pressed forward again eagerly, parting the branches, — speaking to each other rarely and in whispers ; the young man going first and Sylvia following, fascinated, a few steps behind, with her gray eyes dark with excitement.

She grieved because the longed-for white heron was elusive, but she did not lead the guest, she only followed, and there was no such thing as speaking first. The sound of her own unquestioned voice would have terrified her, — it was hard enough to answer yes or no when there was need of that. At last evening began to fall, and they drove the cow home together, and Sylvia smiled with pleasure when they came to the place where she heard the whistle and was afraid only the night before.

HALF a mile from home, at the farther edge of the woods, where the land was highest, a great pine-tree stood, the last of its

generation. Whether it was left for a boundary mark, or for what reason, no one could say; the woodchoppers who had felled its mates were dead and gone long ago, and a whole forest of sturdy trees, pines and oaks and maples, had grown again. But the stately head of this old pine towered above them all and made a landmark for sea and shore miles and miles away. Sylvia knew it well. She had always believed that whoever climbed to the top of it could see the ocean; and the little girl had often laid her hand on the great rough trunk and looked up wistfully at those dark boughs that the wind always stirred, no matter how hot and still the air might be below. Now she thought of the tree with a new excitement, for why, if one climbed it at break of day, could not one see all the world, and easily discover whence the white heron flew, and mark the place, and find the hidden nest ?

What a spirit of adventure, what wild ambition! What fancied triumph and delight and glory for the later morning when she could make known the secret! It was almost too real and too great for the childish heart to bear.

All night the door of the little house

stood open, and the whippoorwills came and sang upon the very step. The young sportsman and his old hostess were sound asleep, but Sylvia's great design kept her broad awake and watching. She forgot to think of sleep. The short summer night seemed as long as the winter darkness, and at last when the whippoorwills ceased, and she was afraid the morning would after all come too soon, she stole out of the house and followed the pasture path through the woods, hastening toward the open ground beyond, listening with a sense of comfort and companionship to the drowsy twitter of a half - awakened bird, whose perch she had jarred in passing. Alas, if the great wave of human interest which flooded for the first time this dull little life should sweep away the satisfactions of an existence heart to heart with nature and the dumb life of the forest!

There was the huge tree asleep yet in the paling moonlight, and small and hopeful Sylvia began with utmost bravery to mount to the top of it, with tingling, eager blood coursing the channels of her whole frame, with her bare feet and fingers, that pinched and held like bird's claws to the monstrous ladder reaching up, up, almost to the sky itself.

First she must mount the white oak tree that grew alongside, where she was almost lost among the dark branches and the green leaves heavy and wet with dew; a bird fluttered off its nest, and a red squirrel ran to and fro and scolded pettishly at the harmless housebreaker. Sylvia felt her way easily. She had often climbed there, and knew that higher still one of the oak's upper branches chafed against the pine trunk, just where its lower boughs were set close together. There, when she made the dangerous pass from one tree to the other, the great enterprise would really begin.

She crept out along the swaying oak limb at last, and took the daring step across into &e

old pine-tree. The way was harder than she thought; sfee-*Hist reach far and hold iaefc, the sharp dry twigs caught and held her and scratched her like angry talons, the pitch made her tfarir~Hlitte fingers clumsy and stiff as she went round and round the tree's great stem, higher and higher upward.^ The sparrows and robins in the woods below were beginning to wake and twitter to the dawn, yet it seemed much lighter there aloft in the pine-tree, and the child knew that she must hurry if her project were to be of any use.

The tree seemed to lengthen itself out as she went up, and to reach farther and farther upward. It was like a great main-mast to the voyaging earth; it must truly have been amazed that morning through all its ponderous frame as it felt this determined spark of human spirit creeping and climbing from higher branch to branch. Who knows how steadily the least twigs held themselves to advantage this light, weak creature on her way! The old pine must have loved his new dependent. More than all the hawks, and bats, and moths, and even the sweet-voiced thrushes, was the brave, beating heart of the solitary gray-eyed child. And the tree stood still and held away the winds that June morning while the dawn grew bright in the east.

Sylvia's face was like a pale star, if one had seen it from the ground, when the last thorny bough was past, and she stood trembling and tired but wholly triumphant, high in the tree-top. Yes, there was the sea with the dawning sun making a golden dazzle over it, and toward that glorious east flew two hawks with slow-moving pinions. How low they looked in the air from that height when before one had only seen them far up,

and dark against the blue sky. Their gray feathers were as soft as moths ; they seemed 7>nly a little way from the tree, and Sylvia felt as if she too could go flying away among the clouds. Westward, the woodlands and farms reached miles and miles into the distance ; here and there were church steeples, and white villages; truly it was a vast and awesome world.

The birds sang louder and louder. At last the sun. came up bewilderingly bright. Sylvia could see the white sails of ships out at sea, and the clouds that were purple and rose-colored and yellow at first began to fade away. Where was the white heron's nest in the sea of green branches, and was this wonderful sight and pageant of the world the only reward for having climbed to such a giddy height? Now look down again, Sylvia, where the green marsh is set among the shining birches and dark hemlocks; there where you saw the white heron once you will see him again ; look, look! a white spot of him like a single floating feather comes up from the dead hemlock and grows larger, and rises, and comes close at last, and goes by the landmark pine with steady sweep of wing and outstretched slender neck and

crested head. And wait! wait! do not move a foot or a finger, little girl, do not send an arrow of light and consciousness from your two eager eyes, for the heron has perched on a pine bough not far beyond yours, and cries back to his mate on the nest, and plumes his feathers for the new day!

The child gives a long sigh a minute later when a company of shouting cat-birds comes also to the tree, and vexed by their fluttering and lawlessness the solemn heron goes away. She knows his secret now, the wild, light, slender bird that floats and wavers, and goes back like an arrow presently to his home in the green world beneath. Then Sylvia, well satisfied, makes her perilous way down again, not daring to look far below the branch she stands on, ready to cry sometimes because her fingers ache and her lamed feet slip. Wondering over and over again what the stranger would say to her, and what he would think when she told him how to find his way straight to the heron's nest.

"Sylvy, Sylvy!" called the busy old grandmother again and again, but nobody answered, and the small husk bed was empty, and Sylvia had disappeared.

The guest waked from a dream, and remembering his day's pleasure hurried to dress himself that it might sooner begin. He was sure from the way the shy little girl looked once or twice yesterday that she had at least seen the white heron, and now she must really be persuaded to tell. Here she comes now, paler than ever, and her worn old frock is torn and tattered, and smeared with pine pitch. The grandmother and the sportsman stand in the door together and question her, and the splendid moment has come to speak of the dead hemlock-tree by the green marsh.

But Sylvia does not speak after all, though the old grandmother fretfully rebukes her, and the young man's kind appealing eyes are looking straight in her own. He can make them rich with money; he has promised it, and they are poor now. He is so well worth making happy, and he waits to hear the story she can tell.

No, she must keep silence! What is it that suddenly forbids her and makes her dumb ? Has she been nine years growing, and now, when the great world for the first

time puts out a hand to her, must she thrust it aside for a bird's sake ? The murmur of the pine's green branches is in her ears, she remembers how the white heron came flying through the golden air and how they watched the sea and the morning together, and Sylvia cannot speak; she cannot tell the heron's secret and give its life away.

Dear loyalty, that suffered a sharp pang as the guest went away disappointed later in the day, that could have served and followed him and loved him as a dog loves ! Many a night Sylvia heard the echo of his whistle haunting the pasture path as she came home with the loitering cow. She forgot even her sorrow at the sharp report of his gun and the piteous sight of thrushes and sparrows dropping silent to the ground, their songs hushed and their pretty feathers stained and wet with blood. Were the birds better friends than their hunter might have been, — who can tell ? Whatever treasures were lost to her, woodlands and summer-time, remember ! Bring your gifts and graces and tell your secrets to this lonely country child!

LAW LANE.

I.

THE thump of a flat-iron signified to an educated passer-by that this was Tuesday morning; yesterday having been fair and the weekly washing-day unhindered by the weather. It was undoubtedly what Mrs. Powder pleased herself by calling a good orthodox week; not one of the disjointed and imperfect sections of time which a rainy Monday forced upon methodical housekeepers. Mrs. Powder was not a woman who could live altogether in the present, and whatever she did was done with a view to having it cleared out of the way of the next enterprise on her list. " I can't bear to see folks do their work as if every piece on 't was a tread-mill," she used to say, briskly. " Life means progriss to me, and I can't dwell by the way no more 'n sparks can fly downwards. 'T ain't the way I 'm built, nor none of the Fisher tribe."

The hard white bundles in the shallow splint-basket were disappearing, one by one, and taking their places on the deerepit clothes-horse, well ironed and precisely folded. The July sunshine came in at one side of Mrs. Powder's kitchen, and the cool northwest breeze blew the heat out again from the other side. Mrs. Powder grew uneasy and impatient as she neared the end of her task, and the flat-iron moved more and more vigorously. She kept glancing out through the doorway and along the country road as if she were watching for somebody.

"I shall just have to git ready an' go an' rout her out myself, an' take my chances," she said at last with a resentful look at the clock, as if it were partly to blame for the delay and had ears with which to listen to proper rebuke. The round moon-face had long ago ceased its waxing and waning across the upper part of the old dial, as if it had forgotten its responsibility about the movements of a heavenly body in its pleased concern about housekeeping.

" See here! " said Mrs. Powder, taking a last hot iron from the fire. " You ain't a-keepiu' time like you used to ; you 're get-tin' lazy, I must say. Look at this 'ere sun-mark on the floor, that calls it full 'leven o'clock, and you want six minutes to ten. I Ve got to send word to the clock-man and have your iu'ards all took apart; you got me to meetin' more 'n half an hour too late, Sabbath last."

To which the moon-face did not change its beaming expression ; very likely, being a moon, it was not willing to mind the ways of the sun.

" Lord, what an old thing you be ! " said Mrs. Powder, turning away with a chuckle. " I don't wonder your sense kind of fails you! " And the clock clucked at her by way of answer, though presently it was going to strike ten at any rate.

The hot iron was now put down hurriedly, and the half-ironed night-cap was left in a queer position on the ironing-board. A small figure had appeared in the road and was coming toward the house with a fleet, barefooted run which required speedy action. " Here you, Joel Smith! " shouted the old woman. " Jo—el! " But the saucy lad only doubled his pace and pretended not to see or hear her. Mrs. Powder could play at that game, too, and did not call again, but quietly went back to her ironing and tried as hard as she could to be provoked. Presently the boy came panting up the slope of green turf which led from the road to the kitchen doorstep.

" I did n't know but you spoke as I ran by," he remarked, in an amiable tone. Mrs. Powder took no heed of him whatever.

" I ain't in no hurry; I kind o' got running," he explained, a moment later; and then, as his hostess stepped toward the stove, he caught up the frilled night-cap and tied it on in a twinkling. When Mrs. Powder turned again, the sight of him was too much for her gravity.

" Them frills is real becoming to ye," she announced, shaking with laughter. " I declare for 't if you don't favor your gran'nia Dodge's looks. I should like to have yer folks see ye. There, take it off now; I 'm most through my ironin' and I want to clear it out o' the way."

Joel was perfectly docile and laid the night-cap within reach. He had a temptation to twitch it back by the end of one string, but he refrained. " Want me to go drive your old brown hen-turkey out o' the wet grass, Mis' Powder ? She's tolling her chicks off down to'a'ds the swamp," he offered.

" She 's raised up families enough to know * how by this time," said Mrs. Powder, " an' the swamp's dry as a bone."

" I '11 split ye up a mess o' kindlin'-wood whilst I 'm here, jest as soon 's not," said Joel, in a still more pleasant tone, after a long and anxious pause.

" There, I '11 get ye your doughnuts, pretty quick. They ain't so fresh as they was Saturday. I s'pose that's what you 're driving at." The good soul shook with laughter. Joel answered as well for her amusement as the most famous of comic actors ; there was something in his appealing eyes, his thin cheeks and monstrous freckles, and his long locks of sandy hair, which was very funny to Mrs. Powder. She was always interested, too, in fruitless attempts to satisfy his appetite. He listened now, for the twentieth time, to her opinion that the bottomless pit alone could be compared to the recesses of his being. " I should like to be able to say that I had filled ye up jest once!" she ended her remarks, as she brought a tin pan full of doughnuts from her pantry.

" Heard the news ? " asked small Joel, as he viewed the provisions with glistening eyes. He bore likeness to a little hungry woodchuck, or muskrat, as he went to work before the tin pan.

" What news ? " Mrs. Powder asked, suspiciously. " I ain't seen nobody this day."

"Barnet's folks has got their ease in court."

" They ain't! " and while a solemn silence fell upon the kitchen, the belated old clock whirred and rumbled and struck ten with persistent effort. Mrs. Powder looked round at it impatiently ; the moon-face confronted her with the same placid smile.

" Twelve o'clock 's the time you git your dinner, ain't it, Mis' Powder ? " the boy inquired, as if he had repeated his news like a parrot and had no further interest in its meaning.

" I don't plot for to get me no reg'lar dinner this day," was the unexpected reply. " You can eat a couple or three o' them nuts and step along, for all I care. An' I want you to go up Lyddy Bangs's lane and carry her word that I 'm goin' out to pick me some blueberries. They '11 be ripened up elegant, and I 've got a longin' for 'em. Tell her I say 't is our day — she '11 know ; we 've be'n after 'arly blueberries together

this forty years, and Lyddy knows where to meet with me; there by them split rocks."

The ironing was finished a few minutes afterward, and the board was taken to its place in the shed. When Mrs. Powder returned, Joel had stealthily departed; the tin pan was turned upside down on the seat of the kitchen chair. " Good land! " said the astonished woman, " I believe he '11 bu'st himself to everlastin' bliss one o' these days. Them doughnuts would have lasted me till Thursday, certain."

" Gimme suthin' to eat, Mis' Powder ? " whined Joel at the window, with his plaintive countenance lifted just above the sill. But he set forth immediately down the road, with bulging pockets and the speed of a light-horseman.

II.

Half an hour later the little gray farmhouse was shut and locked, and its mistress was crossing the next pasture with a surprisingly quick step for a person of her age and weight. An old cat was trotting after her, with tail high in the air, but it was plain to see that she still looked for danger, having

just come down from the woodpile, where she had retreated on Joel's first approach. She kept as close to Mrs. Powder as was consistent with short excursions after crickets or young, unwary sparrows, and opened her wide green eyes fearfully on the lookout for that evil monster, the boy.

There were two pastures to cross, and Mrs. Powder was very much heated by the noonday sun and entirely out of breath when she approached the familiar rendezvous and caught sight of her friend's cape-bonnet.

" Ain't there no justice left ? " was her indignant salutation. " I s'pose you 've heard that Crosby's folks have lost their case? Poor Mis' Crosby! 'twill kill her, I 'm sure. I 've be'n calculatin' to go ber-ryin' all the forenoon, but I could n't git word to you till Joel came tootin' by. I thought likely you 'd expect notice when you see what a good day 't was."

" I did," replied Lyddy Bangs, in a tone much more serious than her companion's. , She was a thin, despairing little body, with an anxious face and a general look of disappointment and poverty, though really the more prosperous person of the two. " Joel

told me you said 't was our day," she added. " I 'm wore out try in' to satisfy that boy; he's always beggin' for somethin' to eat every time he comes nigh the house. I should think they'd see to him to home; not let him batten on the neighbors so."

"You ain't been feedin' of him, too?" laughed Mrs. Powder. " Well, I declare, I don't see whar he puts it! " and she fanned herself with her apron. "I always forget what a sightly spot this is."

"Here's your pussy - cat, ain't she ? " asked Lyddy Bangs, needlessly, as they sat looking off over the valley. Behind them the hills rose one above another, with their bare upland clearings and great stretches of pine and beech forest. Beyond the wide valley was another range of hills, green and pleasant in the clear mid-day light. Some higher mountains loomed, sterile and stony, to northward. They were on the women's right as they sat looking westward.

"It does seem as if folks might keep the peace when the Lord's give 'em so pooty a a spot to live in," said Lyddy Bangs, regretfully. " There ain't no better farms than Baruet's and Crosby's folks have got neither, but 'stead o' neighboring they must

pick their mean fusses and fight from generation to generation. My grau'ma'am used to say 't was just so with 'em when she was a girl — and she was one of the first settlers up this way. She al'ays would have it that Barnet's folks was the most to blame, but there : s plenty sides with 'em, as you know."

" There, 't is all mixed up, so 't is — a real tangle," answered Mrs. Powder. " I 've been o' both minds — I must say I used to hold for the Crosbys in the old folks' time, but I 've come round to see they ain't perfect. There! I 'm b'ilin' over with some-thin' I've got to tell somebody. I've kep' it close long 's I can."

" Let's get right to pickin', then," said Lyddy Bangs, " or we sha'u't budge from here the whole livin' afternoon," and the small thin figure and the tall stout one moved off together toward their well-known harvest-fields. They were presently settled down within good hearing distance, and yet the discussion was not begun. The cat curled herself for a nap on the smooth top of a rock.

" There, I have to eat a while first, like a young-one," said Mrs. Powder. " I always tell 'em that blueberries is only fit to eat

right off of the twigs. You want 'em full o' sun; let 'em git cold and they 're only fit to cook — not but what I eat 'em any ways I can git 'em. Ain't they nice an' spicy? Law, my poor knees is so stiff! I begin to be afraid, nowadays, every year o' berryin' may be my last. I don' know why 't should be that my knees serves me so. I ain't rheumaticky, nor none o' my folks was; we go off with other complaints."

" The mukis membrane o' the knees gits dried up," explained Lyddy Bangs, "an' the j'iuts is all powder-posted. So I 've be'n told, anyways."

" Then they was ignorant," retorted her companion, sharply. " I know by the feelin's I have " — and the two friends picked industriously and discussed the vexed points of medicine no more.

" I can't force them Barnets and Crosbys out o' my mind," suggested Miss Bangs after a while, being eager to receive the proffered confidence which might be forgotten. " Think of 'em, without no other door-neighbors, fightin' for three ginerations over the bounds of a lane wall. What if 't was two foot one way or two foot t'other, let 'em agree."

" But that's just what they could n't," said Mrs. Powder. "You know youi-df you might be willin' to give away a piece o' land, but when somebody said 't wa'n't yours, 't was theirs, 't would take more Christian grace 'n I 've got to let 'em see I thought they was right. All the old Crosbys ever wanted, first, was for the Barnets to say two foot of the lane was theirs by rights, and then they was willin' to turn it into the lane and to give that two foot more o' the wedth than Barnets did — they wa'u't haggling for no pay ; 't was for rights. But Barnet's folks said " —

"Now, don't you go an' git all flustered up a-telliu' that over, Harri't Powder," said the lesser woman. "There ain't be'n no words spoke so often as them along this sidelin' hill, not even the Ten Commandments. The only sense there 's be'n about it is, they 've let each other alone altogether, and ain't spoke at all for six months to a time. I can't help hoping that the war '11 die out with the old breed and they '11 come to some sort of peace. Mis' Barnet was a Sands, and they 're toppin' sort o' folks and she's got fight in her. I think she 's more to blame than Barnet, a good sight; but

Mis' Crosby's a downright peace-making little creatur', and would have ended it long ago if she 'd be'n able."

" Barnet's stubborn, too, let me tell you ! " and Mrs. Powder's voice was full of anger. " 'T will never die out in his day, and he '11 spend every cent lawing, as the old folks did afore him. The lawyers must laugh at him well, 'mongst themselves. One an' another o' the best on 'em has counseled them to leave it out to referees, and tried to show 'em they was fools. My man talked with judge himself about it, once, after he 'd been settin' on a jury and they was comin' away from court. They could n't agree; they never could ! All the spare money o' both farms has gone to pay the lawyers and carry on one fight after another. Now folks don't know it, but Crosby's farm is all mortgaged ; they 've spent even what Mis' Crosby had from her folks. An' there 's worse behind — there 's worse behind," insisted the speaker, stoutly. "I went up there this spring, as you know, when Mis' Crosby was at death's door with lung-fever. I went through everything fetchin' of her round, and was there five weeks, till she pot about. feel to'a'ds you as an own sister,' says

Abby Crosby to me. I 'm a neighboring woman at heart,' says she; ' and just you think of it, that my man had to leave me alone, sick as I was, while he went for you and the doctor, not riskin' to ask Barnet's folks to send for help. I like to live pleasant,' says she to me, and bu'st right out a-cryin'. I knew then how she 'd felt things all these years. — How are they ever goin' to pay more court bills and all them piles o' damages, if the farm's mortgaged so heavy ? " she resumed. " Crosby's farm ain't worth a good two thirds of Barnet's. They 've both neglected their lands. How many you got so fur, Lyddy ? "

Lyddy proudly displayed her gains of blueberries ; the pail was filling very fast, i and the friends were at their usual game of rivalry. Mrs. Powder had been the faster picker in years past, and she now doubled her diligence.

" Ain't the sweet-fern thick an' scented as ever you see ? " she said. " Gimme pas-tui-e-lands rather 'n the best gardins that grows. If I can have a sweet-brier bush and sweet-fern patch and some clumps o' bayberry, you can take all the gardin blooms. Look how folks toils with witch-grass and

pusley and gets a starved lot o' poor sprigs, slug-eat, and all dyin' together in their front yards, when they might get better comfort in the first pasture along the road. I guess there's somethin' wild, that 's never got tutored out o' me. I must ha' be'n made o' somethin' counter to town dust. I never could see why folks wanted to go off an' live out o' sight o' the mountings, an' have everything on a level."

" You said there was worse to tell behind," suggested Lyddy Bangs, as if it were only common politeness to show an appreciation of the friendly offering.

" I have it in mind to get round to that in proper course," responded Mrs. Powder, a trifle offended by the mild pertinacity. " I settled it in my mind that I was goin' to tell you somethin' for a kind of a treat the day we come out blueberryin'. There ! " — and Mrs. Powder rose with difficulty from her knees, and retreated pompously to the shade of a hemlock-tree which grew over a shelving rock near by.

Lyddy Bangs could not resist picking a little longer in an unusually fruitful spot; then she hastened to seat herself by her friend. It was no common occasion.

Mrs. Powder was very warm ; and further evaded and postponed telling the secret by wishing that she were as light on foot as her companion, and deploring her increasing weight. Then she demanded a second sight of the blueberries, which were compared and decided upon as to quality and quantity. Then the cat, which had been left at some distance 011 her rock, came trotting toward her mistress in a disturbed way, and after a minute of security in a comfortable lap darted away again in a strange, excited manner.

" She 's goin' to have a fit, I do believe!" exclaimed Lyddy Bangs, quite disheartened, for the cat was Mrs. Powder's darling and she might leave everything to go in search of her.

" She may have seen a snake or something. She often gets scared and runs home when we 're out a-trarvelin'," said the cat's owner, complacently, and Lyddy's spirits rose again.

" I suppose you never suspected that Ezra Barnet and Ruth Crosby cared the st thing about one another ?" inquired the keeper of the secret a moment later, and the listener turned toward Mrs. Powder with a startled face.

"Now, Harri't Powder, for mercy's sakes alive ! " was all that she could say; but Mrs. Powder was satisfied, and confirmed the amazing news by a most emphatic nod.

" My lawful sakes! what be they goin' to do about it ? " inquired Lyddy Bangs, flushing with excitement. " A Barnet an' a Crosby fall in love ! Don't you rec'lect how the old ones was al'ays fightin' and callin' names when we was all to school together? Times is changed, certain."

" Now, say you hope to die if ever you '11 tell a word I say," pursued Mrs. Powder. " If I was to be taken away to-morrow, you 'd be all the one that would know it except Mis' Crosby and Ezra and Ruth themselves. 'T was nothin' but her bein' nigh to death that urged her to tell me the state o' things. I s'pose she thought I might favor 'em in time to come. Abby Crosby she says to me,' Mis' Powder, my poor girl may need your motherin' care.' An' I says, ' Mis' Crosby, she shall have it;' and then she had a spasm o' pain, and we harped no more that day as I remember."

" How come it about ? I should n't have told anybody that asked me that a Barnet and a Crosby ever 'changed the time o' day,
much less kep' company," protested the listener.

" Kep' company! pore young creatur's ! " said Mrs. Powder. " They 've hid 'em away in the swamps an' hollers, and in the edge o' the growth, at nightfall, for the sake o' git-tin' a word; an' they 've stole out, shiverin', into that plaguy lane o' winter nights. I tell ye I 've heard hifalutin' folks say that love would still be lord of all, but I never was 'strained to believe it till I see what that boy and girl was willin' to undergo. All the hate of all their folks is turned to love ill them, and I couldn't help a-watchiu' of 'em. An' I ventured to send Ruth over to my house after my alpaccy aprin, and then I made an arrant out to the spring-brook to see if there was any cresses started — which I knew well enough there was n't — and I spoke right out bold to Ezra, that was at work on a piece of ditching over on his land. 4 Ezra,' says I, ' if you git time, just run over to the edge o' my pasture and pick me a handful o' balm o' Gilead buds. I want to put 'em in half a pint o' new rum for Mis' Crosby, and there ain't a soul to send.' I knew he 'd just meet her coming back, if I could time it right gittin' of Ruth started.

He looked at me kind of curi's, and pretty quick I see him leggin' it over the fields with an axe and a couple o' ends o' board, like he 'd got to mend a fence. I had to keep her dinner warm for her till ha'-past one o'clock. I don't know what he mentioned to his folks, but Ruth she come an' kissed me hearty when she first come inside the door. 'T is harder for Ezra; he ain't got nobody to speak to, and Ruth's got her mother if she is a Mis' Much-afraid."

" I don't know's we can blame Crosby for not wantin' to give his girl to the Bar-nets, after they 've got away all his substance, his means, an' his cattle, like 't was in the Book o' Job," urged Lyddy Bangs. " Seems as if they might call it square an' marry the young folks off, but they won't nohow; 't will only fan the flame." Lyddy Bangs was a sentimental person ; neighbor Powder had chosen wisely in gaining a new friend to the cause of Ezra Barnet's apparently hopeless affection. Unknown to herself, however, she had been putting the lover's secret to great risk of untimely betrayal.

The weather was most beautiful that afternoon ; there was an almost intoxicating freshness and delight among the sweet odors of the hillside pasture, and the two elderly women were serene at heart and felt like girls again as they talked together. They remembered many an afternoon like this; they grew more and more confiding as they reviewed the past and their life-long friendship. A stranger might have gathered only the most rural and prosaic statements, and a tedious succession of questions, from what Mrs. Powder and Lyddy Bangs had to say to each other, but the old stories of true love and faithful companionship were again simply rehearsed. Those who are only excited by more complicated histories too often forget that there are no new plots to the comedies and tragedies of life. They are played sometimes by country people in homespun, sometimes by townsfolk in velvet and lace. Love and prosperity, death and loss and misfortune—the stories weave themselves over and over again, never mind whether the ploughman or the wit of the clubs plays the part of hero.

The two homely figures sat still so long that they seemed to become permanent points in the landscape, and the sinull birds, and even a wary chipmunk, went their ways unmindful of Mrs. Powder and Lyddy Bangs. The old hemlock-tree, under which they sat discoursing, towered high above the young pine-growth which clustered thick behind them on the hillside. In the middle of a comfortable reflection upon the Barnet grandfather's foolishness or craftiness, Mrs. Powder gave sudden utterance to the belief that some creature up in the tree was dropping pieces of bark and cones all over her.

" A squirrel, most like," said Lyddy Bangs, looking up into the dense branches. " The tree is a-scatterin' down, ain't it ? As you was sayin', Grandsir Barnet must have knowed well enough what he was about" —

" Oh, gorry! oh, git out! ovv — o — w! " suddenly wailed a voice overhead, and a desperate scramble and rustling startled the good women half out of their wits. " Ow, Mis' Powder! " shrieked a familiar voice, while both hearts thumped fast, and Joel came, half falling, half climbing, down out of the tree. He bawled, and beat his head with his hands, and at last rolled in agony among the bayberry and lamb-kill. " Look out for 'em ! " he shouted. " Oh, gorry ! I thought't was only an old last-year's hornet's nest — they '11 sting you, too ! "

Mrs. Powder untied her apron and laid about her with sure aim. Only two hornets were to be seen; but after these were beaten to the earth, and she stopped to regain her breath, Joel hardly dai'ed to lift his head or to look about him.

" What was you up there for, anyhow ? " asked Lyddy Bangs, with severe suspicion. "Harking to us, I'll be bound!" But Mrs. Powder, who knew Joel's disposition best, elbowed her friend into silence and began to inquire about the condition of his wounds. There was a deep-seated hatred between Joel and Miss Bangs.

" Oh, dear! they 've bit me all over," groaned the boy. " Ain't you got soniethiu' you can rub on, Mis' Powder?" — and the rural remedy of fresh earth was suggested.

" 'T is too dry here," said the adviser. "Just you step down to that ma'shy spot there by the brook, dear, and daub you with the wet mud real good, and 't will ease you right away." Mrs. Powder's voice sounded i/ compassionate, but her spirit and temper of mind gave promise of future retribution.

" I teach him to follow us out eavesdropping, this fashion! " said Lyddy Bangs, when the boy had departed, weeping. " I 'm

more 'n gratified that the hornets got hold of him! I hope 't will serve him for a lesson."

" Don't you r'ile him up one mite, now," pleaded Mrs. Powder, while her eyes bore witness of hardly controlled anger. " He 's the worst tattle-tale I ever see, and we 've put ourselves into a trap. If he tells his mother she '11 spread it all over town. But I should no more thought o' his bein' up in that tree than o' his bein' the sarpent in the garden o' Eden. You leave Joel to me, and be mild with him 's you can."

The culprit approached, still lamenting. His ear and cheek were hugely swollen already, so that one eye was nearly closed. The blueberry expedition was relinquished, and with heavy sighs of dissatisfaction Lyddy Bangs took up the two half-filled pails, while Mrs. Powder kindly seized Joel by his small, thin hand, and the little group moved homeward across the pasture.

" Where's your hat ? " asked Lyddy, stopping short, after they had walked a little distance.

" Hanging on a limb up by the wop's nest," answered Joel. " Oh, git me home, Mis' Powder! "

III.

No one would suspect, from the look of the lane itself, that it had always been such a provoker of wrath, and even a famous battle-ground. While petty wars had raged between the men and women of the old farms, walnut-trees had grown high in air, and apple-trees had leaned their heavy branches on the stone walls and, year after year, decked themselves in pink-and-white blossoms to arch this unlucky by-way for a triumphal procession of peace that never came. Birds built their nests in the boughs and pecked the ripe blackberries; green brakes and wild roses and tall barberry-bushes flourished in their season on either side the wheel-ruts. It was a remarkably pleasant country lane, where children might play and lovers might linger. No one would imagine that this lane had its lawsuits and damages, its annual crop of briefs, and succession of surveyors and quarrelsome partisans ; or that in every generation of owners each man must be either plaintiff or defendant.

The surroundings looked permanent enough. No one would suspect that a certain piece of wall had been more than once thrown clown by night and built again, angrily, by day; or that a well-timbered corn-house had been the cause of much litigation, and even now looked, when you came to know its story, as if it stood on its long, straight legs, like an ungainly, top-heavy beast, all ready to stalk away when its position became too dangerous. The Barnets had built it beyond their boundary; it had been moved two or three times, backward and forward.

The Barnet house and land stood between the Crosby farm and the high-road; the Crosbys had never been able to reach the highway without passing their enemies under full fire of ugly looks or taunting voices. The intricacies of legal complications in the matter of right of way would be impossible to explain. They had never been very clear to any impartial investigator. Barnets and Crosbys had gone to their graves with bitter hatred and sullen desire for revenge in their hearts. Perhaps this one great interest, outside the simple matters of food and clothing and farmers' work, had taken the place to them of drama and literature and art. One could not help thinking, as he looked at the decrepit fences and mossy, warped roofs and buckling walls, to how much better use so much money might have been put. The costs of court and the lawyers' fees had taken everything, and men had drudged, in heat and frost, and women had pinched and slaved to pay the lane's bills. Both the Barnet and Crosby of the present time stood well enough in the opinion of other neighbors. They were hard-fisted, honest men; the fight was inherited to begin with, and they were stubborn enough to hold fast to the fight. Law Lane was as well known as the county roads in half a dozen towns. Perhaps its irreconcilable owners felt a thrill of enmity that had come straight down from Scottish border-frays, as they glanced along its crooked length. Who could believe that the son and daughter of the warring households, instead of being ready to lift the torch in their turn, had weakly and misguidedly fallen in love with each other ? Nobody liked Mrs. Barnet. She was a cross-grained, suspicious soul, who was a tyrant and terror of discomfort in her own household whenever the course of events ran counter to her preference. Her son Ezra was a complete contrast to her in disposition,

and to his narrow-minded, prejudiced father as well. The elder Ezra was capable of better things, however, and might have been reared to friendliness and justice, if the Crosby of his youthful day had not been specially aggravating and the annals of Law Lane at their darkest page. If there had been another boy to match young Ezra, on the Crosby farm, the two might easily have fostered their natural boyish rivalries until something worse came into being; but when one's enemy is only a sweet-faced little girl, it is very hard to impute to her all manner of discredit and serpent-like power of evil. At least, so Ezra Barnet the younger felt in his inmost heart; and though he minded his mother for the sake of peace, and played his solitary games and built his unapplauded dams and woodchuck - traps on his own side of the fences, he always saw Ruth Crosby as she came and went, and liked her better and better as years went by. When the tide of love rose higher than the young people's steady heads, they soon laid fast hold of freedom. With all their perplexities, life was by no means at its worst, and rural diplomacy must bend all its energies to hinder these unexpected lovers.

Ezra Barnet had never so much as entered the Crosby house ; the families were severed beyond the reuniting power of even a funeral. E/ra could only try to imagine the room to which his Ruth had returned one summer evening after he had left her, reluctantly, because the time drew near for his father's return from the village. His mother had been in a peculiarly bad temper all day, and he had been glad to escape from her unwelcome insistence that he should marry any one of two or three capable girls, and so furnish some help in the housekeeping. Ezra had often heard this suggestion of his duty, and, tired and provoked at last, he had stolen out to the garden and wandered beyond it to the brook and out to the fields. Somewhere, somehow, he had met Ruth, and the lovers bewailed their trials with unusual sorrow and impatience. It seemed very hard to wait. Young Barnet was ready to persuade the tearful girl that they must go away together and establish a peaceful home of their own. He was heartily ashamed because the last verdict was in his father's favor, and Ruth forebore to wound him with any glimpse of the straits to which her own father had been reduced. She was

too dutiful to leave the pinched household, where her help was needed more than ever; she persuaded her lover that they were sure to be happy at last — indeed, were not they happy now ? How much worse it would be if they could not safely seize so many opportunities, brief though they were, of being together! If the fight had been less absorbing and the animosity less bitter, they might-have been suspected long ago.

So Ruth and Ezra parted, with uncounted kisses, and Ezra went back to the dingy-walled kitchen, where his mother sat alone. It was hardly past twilight out of doors, but Mrs. Barnet had lighted a kerosene-lamp, and sat near the small open window mending a hot-looking old coat. She looked so needlessly uncomfortable and surly that her son was filled with pity, as he stood watching her, there among the moths and beetles that buffeted the lamp-chimney.

" Why don't you put down your sewing and come out a little ways up the road, mother, and get cooled off ?" he asked, pleasantly ; but she only twitched herself in her chair and snapped off another needleful of linen thread.

" I can't spare no time to go gallivantin',

like some folks," she answered. " I always have had to work, and I always shall. I see that Crosby girl mincin' by an hour ago, as if she 'd be'ii oft' all the afternoon. Folks that think she 's so amiable about saving her mother's strength would be surprised at the way she dawdles round, I guess " — and Mrs. Barnet crushed an offending beetle with her brass thimble in a fashion that disgusted Ezra. Somehow, his mother had a vague instinct that he did not like to hear ^/ sharp words about Ruth Crosby. Yet he rarely had been betrayed into an ill-judged defense. He had left Ruth only a minute ago; he knew exactly what she had been doing all day, and from what kind errand she had been returning; the blood rushed quickly to his face, and he rose from his seat by the table and went out to the kitchen doorstep. The air was cool and sweet, and a sleepy bird chirped once or twice from an elm-bough overhead. The moon was near its rising, and he could see the great shapes of the mountains that lay to the eastward. He forgot his mother, and began to think about Ruth again ; he wondered if she were not thinking of him, and meant to ask her if she remembered an especial feeling of

nearness just at this hour. Ezra turned to look at the clocks to mark the exact time.

" Yes," said Mrs. Barnet, as she saw him try to discover the hour, " 't is time that father was to home. I s'pose, bein' mail-night, everybody was out to the post-office to hear the news, and most like he 's bawlin' himself hoarse about fall 'lections or something. He ain't got done braggin' about our gittin' the case, neither. There's always some new one that wants to git the p'ints right from headquarters. I didn't see Crosby go by, did you ? "

" He 'd have had to foot it by the path 'cross-lots," replied Ezra, gravely, from the doorstep. " He 's sold his hoss."

" He ain't!" exclaimed Mrs. Barnet, with a chuckle. " I s'pose they 're proddin' him for the money up to court. Guess he won't try to fight us again for one while."

Ezra said nothing; he could not bear this sort of thing much longer. " I won't be kept like a toad under a harrow," he muttered to himself. "I think it seems kind of hard," he ventured to say aloud. " Now he 's got to hire when fall work comes on, and " —

The hard-hearted woman within had long

been trying to provoke her peaceable son into an argument, and now the occasion had come. Ezra restrained himself from speech with a desperate e,ffort, and stopped his ears to the sound of his mother's accusing voice. In the middle of her harangue a wagon was driven into the yard, and his father left it quickly and came toward the door.

" Come in here, you lout! " he shouted, angrily. " I want to look at you ! I want to see what such a mean-spirited sneak has got to say for himself." Then changing his voice to a whine, he begged Ezra, who had caught him from falling as he stumbled over the step, " Come in, boy, an' tell me 't ain't true. I guess they was only thornin' of me up; you ain't took a shine to that Crosby miss, now, have you ? "

" No son of mine — no son of mine ! " burst out the mother, who had been startled by the sudden entrance of the news-bringer. Her volubility was promptly set free, and Ezra looked from his father's face to his mother's.

" Father," said he, turning away from the scold, who was nearly inarticulate in her excess of rage — " father, I 'd rather talk to you, if you want to hear what I 've got to say. Mother 's got no reason in her."

" Ezry," said the elder man, " I see how 't is. Let your ma'am talk all she will. I 'm broke with shame of ye ! " — his voice choked weakly in his throat. " Either you tell me 't is all nonsense, or you go out o' that door and shut it after you for good. An' ye 're all the boy I 've got."

The woman had stopped at last, mastered by the terror of the moment. Her hus-band's face was gray with passion ; her son's cheeks were flushed and his eyes were full of tears. Mrs. Barnet's tongue for once had lost its cunning.

The two men looked at each other as long as they could; the younger man's eyes fell first. " I wish you would n't be hasty," he said ; " to-morrow " —

" You 've heard," was the only answer ; and in a moment more Ezra Barnet reached to the table and took his old straw hat which lay there.

" Good-by, father!" he said, steadily. " I think you 're wrong, sir; but I never meant to carry on that old fight and live like the heathen." And then, young and strong and angry, he left the kitchen.

" He might have took some notice o' me, if he 's goin' for good," said the mother spitefully; but her son did not hear this taunt, and the father only tottered where he stood. The moths struck against his face as if it were a piece of wood; he sank feebly into a chair, muttering, and trying to fortify himself in his spent anger.

Ezra went out, dazed and giddy. But he found the young horse wandering about the yard, eager for his supper and fretful at the strange delay. He unharnessed the creature and backed the wagon under the shed; then he turned and looked at the house — should he go in ? No! The fighting instinct, which had kept firm grasp on father and grandfather, took possession of Ezra now. He crossed the yard and went out at the gate, and down the lane's end to the main road. The father and mother listened to his footsteps, and the man gave a heavy groan.

"Let him go—let him go! 'twill teach him a lesson! " said Mrs. Barnet, with something of her usual spirit. She could not say more, though she tried her best; the occasion was far too great.

How many times that summer Mrs. Powder attempted to wreak vengeance upon Joel, the tattle-tale; into what depths of in-termittent remorse the mischief-making boy was resolutely plunged, who shall describe ? No more luncheons of generous provision ; no more jovial skirmishing at the kitchen windows, or liberal payment for easy errands. Whenever Mrs. Powder saw Lyddy Bangs, or any other intimate and sympathetic friend, she bewailed her careless confidences under the hemlock-tree and detailed her anxious attentions to the hornet-stung eavesdropper.

" I went right home," she would say, sorrowfully ; " I filled him plumb-full with as good a supper as I could gather up, and I took all the fire out o' them hornit-stings with the best o' remedies. ' Joel, dear,' says I, 'you won't lose by it if you keep your mouth shut about them words I spoke to Lyddy Bangs,' and he was that pious I might ha' known he meant mischief. They ain't boys nor men, they're divils, when they come to that size, and so you mark my words! But his mother never could keep nothing to herself, and I knew it from past sorrers ; and I never slept a wink that night — sure 's you live — till the roosters crowed for day." " Perhaps 't won't do nothin' but good ! "

Lyddy Bangs would say, consolingly. " Perhaps the young folks '11 git each other a sight the sooner. They 'd had to kep' it to theirselves till they was gray-headed, 'less somebody let the cat out o' the bag."

" Don't you rec'lect how my cat acted that day! " exclaimed Mrs. Powder, excitedly. "

How she was good as took with a fit! She knowed well enough what was brewin'; I only wish we 'd had half of her

IV.

The day before Christmas all the long valley was white with deep, new-fallen snow. The road which led up from the neighboring village and the railroad station stretched along the western slope — a mere trail, untrodden and unbroken. The storm had just ceased ; the high mountain-peaks were clear and keen and rose-tinted with the waning light; the hills were no longer green with their covering of pines and maples and beeches, but gray with bare branches, and a cold, dense color, almost black, where the evergreens grew thickest. On the other side of the valley the farmsteads were

mapped out as if in etching or pen-drawing; the far-away orchards were drawn with a curious exactness and regularity, the crooked boughs of the apple-trees and the longer lines of the walnuts and ashes and elms came out against the snow with clear beauty. The fences and walls were buried in snow; the farm-houses and barns were petty shapes in their right-angled unlikeness to natural growths. You were half amused, half shocked, as the thought came to you of indifferent creatures called men and women, who busied themselves within those narrow walls, under so vast a sky, and fancied the whole importance of the universe was belittled by that of their few pent acres. What a limitless world lay outside those plaything-farms, yet what beginnings of immortal things the small gray houses had known!

The day before Christmas ! — a festival which seemed in that neighborhood to be of modern origin. The observance of it was hardly popular yet among the elder people, but Christmas had been appropriated, nevertheless, as if everybody had felt the lack of it. New Year's Day never was sufficient for New England, even in its least mirthful

decades. For those persons who took true joy in life, something deeper was needed than the spread-eagle self-congratulations of the Fourth of July, or the family reunions of Thanksgiving Day. There were no bells ringing which the country-folks in Law Lane might listen for on Christmas Eve; but something more than the joy that is felt in the poorest dwelling when a little child, with all its possibilities, is born; something happier still came through that snowy valley with the thought of a Christmas-Child who "was the bringer-in and founder of the reign of the higher life." This was the greater Thanksgiving Day, when the whole of Christendom is called to praise and prny and hear the good-tidings, and every heart catches something of the joyful inspirations of good-will to men.

Ezra Barnet sat on a fallen tree from which he had brushed the powdery snow. It was hard work wading through the drifts, and he had made good headway up the long hill before he stopped to rest. Across the valley in the fading daylight he saw the two farms, and could even trace the course of Law Lane itself, marked by the well-known trees.

How small his own great nut-tree looked at this distance! The two houses, with their larger and smaller out-buildings and snow-topped woodpiles, looked as if they had crept near together for protection and companionship. There were no other houses within a wide space. Ezra knew how remote the homes really were from each other, judged by any existing sympathy and interest. He thought of his bare, unnourished boyhood with something like resentment; then he remembered how small had been his parents' experience, what poor ambition had been fostered in them by their lives ; even his mother's impatience with the efforts he had made to bring a little more comfort and pleasantness to the old farm-house was thought of with pity for her innate lack of pleasure in pleasant things. Ezra himself was made up of inadequacies, being born and bred of the Barnets. He was at work on the railroad now, with small pay; but he had always known that there could be something better than the life in their farmhouse, while his mother did not. A different feeling came over him as he thought whom the other farm - house sheltered; he had looked for that first, to see if it were stand-

ing safe. Ruth's last letter had come only tlif day before. This Christmas holiday was to be a surprise to her. lie wondered whether Ruth's father would let him in.

Never mind! he could sleep in the barn among the hay ; and Ezra dropped into the snow again from the old tree-trunk and went his way. There was a small house just past a bend in the road, and he quickened his steps toward it. Alas ! there was no smoke in Mrs. Powder's chimney. She was away on one of her visiting tours ; nursing some sick person, perhaps. She would have housed him for the night most gladly ; now he must take his chances in Law Lane.

The darkness was already beginning to fall; there was a curious brownness in the air, like summer twilight; the cold air became sharper, and the young man shivered a little as he walked. He could not follow the left-hand road, where it led among hospitable neighbors, but turned bravely off toward his old home — a long, lonely walk at any time of the year, among woods and thickets all well known to him, and as familiar as they were to the wild creatures that haunted them. Yet Ezra Barnet did not find it easy to whistle as he went along.

Suddenly, from behind a scrub-oak that was heavily laden with dead leaves and snow, leaped a small figure, and Ezra was for the moment much startled. The boy carried a rabbit-trap with unusual care, and placed it on the snow-drift before which he stood waist-deep already. " Gorry, Ezry! you most scared me to pieces ! " said Joel, in a perfectly calm tone. " Wish you Merry Christmas ! Folks '11 be lookin' for you ; they did n't s'pose you 'd git home before to-morrow, though."

" Looking for me ? " repeated the young man, with surprise. " I did n't send no word " —
" Ain't you heard nothin' 'bout your ma'am's being took up for dead ? "

"No, I ain't; and you ain't foolin' me with your stories, Joel Smith ? You need n't play off any of your mischief onto me."

" What you gittin' mad with me about ? " inquired Joel, with a plaintive tone in his voice. " She got a fall out in the barn this mornin', an' it liked to killed her. Most folks ain't heard nothin' 'bout it 'cause its been snowin' so. They come for Mis' Powder and she called out to our folks, as they brought her round by the way of Asa Pack-er's store to git some opodildack or some-thin'."

Ezra asked no more questions, but strode past the boy, who looked after him a moment, and then lifted the heavy box-trap and started homeward. The imprisoned rabbit had been snowed up since the day before at least, and Joel felt humane anxieties, else he would have followed Ezra at a proper distance and learned something of his reception.

Mrs. Powder was reigning triumphant in the Barnet house, being nurse, housekeeper, and spiritual adviser all in one. She had been longing for an excuse to spend at least half a day under that cheerless roof for many months, but occasion had not offered. She found the responsibility of the parted lovers weighing more and more heavily on her mind, and had set her strong will at work to find some way of reuniting them, and even to restore a long-banished peace to the farms. She would not like to confess that a mild satisfaction caused her heart to feel warm and buoyant when an urgent summons had come at last; but such was the simple truth. A man who had been felling

trees on the farm brought the news, melancholy to hear under other circumstances, that Mrs. Barnet had been hunting eggs in a stray nest in the hay-mow, and had slipped to the floor and been taken up insensible. Bones were undoubtedly broken ; she was a heavy woman, and had hardly recovered her senses. The doctor must be found as soon as possible. Mrs. Powder hastily put her house to rights, and, with a good round bundle of what she called her needments, set forth on the welcome enterprise. On the way she could hardly keep herself from undue cheerfulness, and if ever there was likely to be a reassuring presence in a sick-room it was Harriet Powder's that December day.

She entered the gloomy kitchen looking like a two-footed snow-drift, her big round shoulders were so heaped with the damp white flakes. Old Ezra Barnet sat by the stove in utter despair, and waved a limp hand warningly toward the bedroom door.

" She's layin' in a sog," he said, hopelessly. " I ought to thought to send word to pore Ezry — all the boy she ever had."

Mrs. Powder calmly removed her snowy outer garments, and tried to warm her hands over the fire.

" Put in a couple o' sticks of good d ry wood," she suggested, in a soothing voirr; and the fanner felt his spirits brighten, he knew not why. Then the whole-souled, hearty woman walked into the bedroom.

"All I could see," she related afterward, " was the end of Jane Barnet's nose, and I was just as sure then as I be now that she was likely to continner; but I set down side of the bed and got holt of her hand, and she groaned two or three times real desperate. I wished the doctor was there, to see if anything really ailed her ; but I someways knowed there wa'n't, 'less 't was gittin' over such a jounce. I spoke to her, but she never said nothin', and I went back out into the kitchen. ' She's a very sick woman,' says I, loud enough for her to hear me ; I knew 't would please her. There was a good deal to do, and I put on my aprin and took right holt and begun to lay about me and git dinner; the men-folks was wiltin' for want o' somethin', it being nigh three o'clock. An' then I got Jane to feel more comfortable with ondressin' of her, for all she 'd hardly let me touch of her — poor creatur', I expect she did feel sore ! — and then daylight was failin' and I felt kind o' spent, so

I set me down in a cheer by the bed-head and was speechless, too. I knew if she was able to speak she could n't hold in no great spell longer.

"After a while she stirred a little and groaned, and then says she, ' Ain't the doctor comin' ?' And I peaced her up well 's I could. 'Be I very bad off, Harri't?' says she.

" ' We hope for the best, Jane,' says I; and that minute the notion come to me how I 'd work her round, an' I like to faughed right out, but I did n't.

" 'If I should lose me again, you must see to sendin' for my son,' says she ; ' his father's got no head.'

" ' I will,' says I, real solemn. ' An' you can trust me with anything you feel to say, sister Barnet.'

" She kind of opened her eye that was next to me and surveyed my countenance sharp, but I looked serious, and she groaned real honest. ' Be I like old Mis' Topliff ?' she whispered, and I kind o' nodded an' put my hand up to my eyes. She was like her, too ; some like her, but not nigh so bad, for Mis' Topliff was hurt so fallin' down the sullar-stairs that she never got over it an' died the day after.

" Oh, my sakes !' she bu'st out whinin', * I can't be took away now. I ain't a-goin' to die right off, be I, Mis' Powder ? '

" I ain't the one to give ye hope. In the midst of life we are in death. We ain't sure of the next minute, none of us,' says I, mean in' it general, but discoursin' away like an old book o' sermons.

" ' I do feel kind o' failin', now,' says she. ' Oh, can't you do nothin' ?' — and I come over an' set on the foot o' the bed an' looked right at her. I knew she was a dreadful notional woman, and always made a fuss when anything was the matter with her; could n't bear no kind o' pain.

" ' Sister Barnet,' says I, ' don't you bear nothin' on your mind you 'd like to see righted before you go ? I know you ain't been at peace with Crosby's folks, and 't ain't none o' my business, but I should n't want to be called away with hard feelin's in my heart. You must overlook my speaking right out, but I sliould want to be so used myself.'

" Poor old creatur' ! She had an awful fight of it, but she beat her temper for once an' give in. 4 I do forgive all them Crosbys,' says she, an' rolled up her eyes. I says to myself that wa'n't all I wanted, but I let her alone a spell, and set there watchin' as if I expected her to breathe her last any minute.

" She asked for Barnet, and I said he was anxious and out watchin' for the doctor, now the snow'd stopped. 'I wish I could see Ezra,' says she. * I 'm all done with the lane now, and I 'd keep the peace if I was goin' to live.' Her voice got weak, and I did n't know but she was worse off than I s'posed. I was scared for a minute, and then I took a grain o' hope. I 'd watched by too many dyin'-beds not to know the difference.

" Don't ye let Barnet git old Nevins to make my coffin, will ye, Mis' Powder ?' says she once.

"' He 's called a good workman, ain't he ? ' says I, soothin' as I could. When it come to her givin' funeral orders, 'twas more 'n I could do to hold in.

" ' I ain't goin' snappin' through torment in a hemlock coffin, to please that old cheat I ' says she, same 's if she was well, an' ris' right up in bed ; and then her bruises pained her an' she dropped back on the pillow.

" ' Oh, I 'm a-goin' now !' says she. ' I 've been an awful hard woman. 'T was I put Barnet up to the worst on't. I 'm willin' Ezra should marry Ruthy Crosby; she 's a nice, pooty gal, and I never owned it till now I 'm on my dyin'-bed — Oh, I 'm ' a-goin', I 'm a-goin'! — Ezra can marry her, and the two farms together '11 make the best farm in town. Barnet ain't got no fight left; he 's like an old sheep since we drove off Ezra.' And then she 'd screech; you never saw no such a fit of narves. And the end was I had to send to Crosby's, in all the snow, for them to come over.

" An; Barnet was got in to hold her hand and hear last words enough to make a Fourth o' July speech ; and I was sent out to the door to hurry up the Crosbys, and who should come right out o' the dark but Ezra. I declare, when I see him you could a-knocked me down with a feather. But I got him by the sleeve — ' You hide away a spell,' says I, ' till I set the little lamp in this winder ; an' don't you make the best o' your ma's condition ; 'pear just as consarned about her as you can. I '11 let ye know why, soon 's we can talk' — and I shoved him right out an' shut the door.

LAW LANE.
207

" The groans was goin' on, and in come Crosby and Ruth, lookin' scared about to death themselves. Neither on 'em had ever been in that house before, as I know of. She called 'em into the bedroom and said she'd had hard feelin's towards them and wanted to make peace before she died, and both on 'em shook hands with her.

" ' Don't you want to tell Ruth what you said to me about her and Ezry?' says I, whisperin' over the bed. ' 'Live or dead, you know 't is right and best.'

"' There ain't no half way 'bout me,' she says, and so there wa'n't. ' Ruth,' says she, out loud, ' I want you to tell pore Ezra that I gave ye both my blessin',' and I made two steps acrost that kitchen and set the lamp in the window, and in comes Ezra — pore boy, he didn't know what was brewin', and thought his mother was dyin' certain when he saw the Crosbys goin' in.

" He went an' stood beside the bed, an' his father clutched right holt of him. Thinks I to myself, if you make as edifyin' an end when your time really does come, you may well be thankful, Jane Barnet!

" They was all a-weepiu', an' I was weepiu' myself, if you'll believe it, I'd got

a-goin' so. You ought to seen her take holt o' Ruth's hand :uf Il/.ia's an' put 'em together. TJien I 'd got all I wanted, I tell you. An' after she'd screeched two or three times more she begun to git tired ; the poor old creatur' was shook up dreadful, and I felt for her consid'able, though you may not think it; so I beckoned 'em out into the kitchen an' went in an' set with her alone. She dropped off into a good easy sleep, an' 1 told the folks her symptoms was more encouragin'.

44 1 tell you, if ever I took handsome care o' any sick person 't was Jane Barnet, before she got about again ; an' Ruth she used to come over an' help real willin'. She got holt of her ma'-in-law's bunnit one afternoon an' trimmed it up real tasty, and that pleased Mis' Barnet about to death. My conscience pricked me some, but not a great sight. I 'm willin' to take what blame come to me by rights.

44 The doctor come postin' along, late that night, and said she was doin' well, owiu' to the care she 'd had, and give me a wink. And she 's alive yet," Mrs. Powder always assured her friends, triumphantly — " and, what's more, is iniddlin' peaceable disposed.

She 's said one or two p'inted things to me, though, an' I should n't wonder, come to think it over, if she mistrusted me just the least grain. But, dear sakes! they never was so comfortable in their lives; an' Ezra he got a first-rate bargain for a lot o' Crosby's woodland that the railroad wanted, and peace is kind o' set in amou'st 'em up in Law Lane."

V.

When Ezra Barnet waked on Christmas morning, in his familiar, dark little chamber under the lean-to roof, he could hardly believe that he was at home again, and that such strange things had happened. There were cheerful voices in the kitchen below, and he dressed hurriedly and went downstairs.

There was Mrs. Powder, cooking the breakfast with lavish generosity, and beaming with good-nature. Barnet, the father, was smiling and looking on with pleased anticipation ; the sick woman was comfortably bolstered up in the bedroom. In all his life the son had never felt so drawn to his mother ; there was a new look in her eyes as

he went toward her ; she had lost her high color, and looked at him pleadingly, as she never had done before. " Ezry, come close here! " said she. " I believe I 'm goin' to git about ag'in, after all. Mis' Powder says I be ; but them feelin's I had .slippin' down the mow, yesterday, was twice as bad as the thump I struck with. I may never be the same to work, but I ain't goin' to fight with folks no more, sence the Lord '11 let me live a spell longer. I ain't a-goin' to fight with nobody, no matter how bad J want to. Now, you go an' git you a good breakfast. I ain't eat a mouthful since breakfast yesterday, and you can bring me a help o' anything Sister Powder favors my havin'."

" I hope 't will last," muttered Sister Powder to herself, as she heaped the blue plate. " Wish you all a Merry Christmas! " she said. " I like to forgot my manners."

It was Christmas Day, whether anybody in Law Lane remembered it or not. The sun shone bright on the sparkling snow, the eaves were dropping, and the snow-birds and blue-jays came about the door. The wars of Law Lane were ended.

A LOST LOVER.

FOR a great many years it had been understood in Longfield that Miss Horatia Dane once had a lover, and that he been lost at sea. By little and little, in one way and another, her acquaintances found out or made up the whole story; and Miss Dane stood in the position, not of an unmarried woman exactly, but rather of having spent most of her life in a long and lonely widowhood. She looked like a person with a history, strangers often said (as if we each did not have a history) ; and her own unbroken reserve about this romance of hers gave everybody the more respect for it.

The Longfield people paid willing deference to Miss Dane: her family had always been one that could be liked and respected and she was the last that was left in the old home of which she was so fond. This was a high, square house, with a row of pointed windows in its roof, a peaked porch in front,

with some lilac-bushes near it; and down by the road was a long, orderly procession of poplars, like a row of sentinels standing guard. She had lived here alone since her father's death, twenty years before. She was a kind, just woman whose pleasures were of a stately and sober sort; and she seemed not unhappy in her loneliness, though she sometimes said gravely that she was the last of her family, as if the fact had a great sadness for her.

She had some middle-aged and elderly cousins who lived at a distance, and they came occasionally to see her ; but there had been no \'7d r oung people staying in her house for many years until this summer, when the daughter of her youngest cousin had written to ask if she might come to make a visit. She was a motherless girl of twenty, both older and younger than her years. Her father and brother, who were civil engineers, had taken some work upon the line of a railway in the far Western country. Nelly had made many long journeys with them before and since she had left school, and she had meant to follow them now, after spending a fortnight with the old cousin whom she had not seen since her childhood.

Her father had laughed at this visit as a freak, and warned her of the dullness and primness of Longfield; but the result was that the girl found herself very happy in the comfortable home. She was still her own free, unfettered, lucky, and sunshiny self; and the old house was so much pleasanter for the girlish face and life, that Miss Ho-ratia had, at first timidly and then most heartily, begged her to stay for the whole summer, or even the autumn, until her father was ready to come East. The name of Dane was very dear to Miss Horatia, and she grew fonder of her guest. When the village people saw her glance at the girl affectionately, as they sat together in the family pew of a Sunday, or saw them walking together after tea, they said it was a good thing for Miss Horatia; how bright she looked! and no doubt she would leave all her money to Nelly Dane, if she played her cards well.

But we will do Nelly justice, and say that she was not mercenary; she would have scorned such a thought. She had grown to have a great love for her cousin Horatia, and really liked to please her. She idealized her, I have no doubt; and her repres-

sion, her grave courtesy and rare words of approval, had a great fascination for a girl who had just been used to people who chattered, and were upon most intimate terms with you directly, and could forget you with equal ease. And Nelly liked having so admiring and easily pleased an audience as Miss Dane and her old servant Melissa. She liked to be queen of her company: she had so many gay, bright stories of what had happened to herself and her friends. Beside, she was clever with her needle, and had all those practical gifts which elderly women approve so heartily in girls. They liked her pretty clothes; she was sensible, and economical, and busy; they praised her to each other and to the world, and even stubborn old Andrew, the man servant to whom Miss Horatia herself spoke with deference, would do anything she asked. Nelly would by no means choose so dull a life as this for the rest of her days; but she enjoyed it immensely for the time being. She instinctively avoided all that would shock the grave dignity and old-school ideas of vX Miss Dane; and somehow she never had felt happier or better satisfied with life. Perhaps it was because she was her best and

most lady-like self. It was not long before she knew the village people almost as well as Miss Dane did, and she became a very great favorite, as a girl so easily can who is good-natured and pretty, and well versed in city fashions; who has the tact and cleverness that come to such a nature from going about the world and knowing many people.

She had not been in Longfield many weeks before she heard something of Miss Dane's love-story ; for one of her new friends asked, in a confidential moment, " Does your cousin ever speak to you about the young man to whom she was engaged to be married ? " And Nelly answered, " No," with great wonder, and not without regret at her own ignorance. After this she kept eyes and ears open for whatever news of this lover's existence might be found.

At last it happened one morning that she had a good chance for a friendly talk with Melissa; for who should know the family affairs better than she ? Miss Horatia had taken her second-best parasol, with a deep fringe, and had gone majestically down the street to do some household errands which she could trust to no one. Melissa was shelling peas at the shady kitchen doorstep,

and Nelly came strolling round from the garden, along the clean-swept flag-stones, and sat down to help her. Melissa moved along, with a grim smile, to make room for her. " You need n't bother yourself," said she. " I 've nothing else to do. You '11 green your fingers all over." But she was evidently pleased to have company.

" My fingers will wash," said Nelly, " and I 've nothing else to do either. Please push the basket this way a little, or I shall scatter the pods, and then you will scold." She went to work busily, while she tried to think of the best way to find out the story she wished to hear.

" There! " said Melissa, " I never told Miss H'ratia to get some citron, and I settled yesterdav to make some pound-cake this forenoon after I got dinner along a piece. She 's most out o' mustard too; she's set about having mustard to eat with her beef, just as the old colonel was before her. I never saw any other folks eat mustard with their roast beef; but every family has their own tricks. I tied a thread round my left-hand little finger purpose to remember that citron before she came down this morning. I hope I ain't losing my fac'lties." It was

seldom that Melissa was so talkative as this at first. She was clearly in a talkative mood.

" Melissa," asked Nelly, with great bravery, after a minute or two of silence, " who was it that my cousin Horatia was going to marry ? It's odd that I should n't know; but I don't remember father's ever speaking of it, and I should n't think of asking her."

" I s'pose it '11 seem strange to you," said Melissa, beginning to shell the peas a great deal faster, " but as many years as I have lived in this house with her, — her mother, the old lady, fetched me up, — I never knew Miss H'ratia to say a word about him. But there! she knows I know, and we 've got an understanding on many things we never talk over as some folks would. I 've heard about it from other folks. She was visiting her great-aunt in Salem when she met with him. His name was Carrick, and it was presumed they was going to be married when he came home from the voyage he was lost on. He had the promise of going out master of a new ship. They did n't keep company long; it was made up of a sudden, and folks here did n't get hold of the story till some time after. I 've heard some that ought to know say it was only talk, and they

never was engaged to be married no more than I ain."

" You say he was lost at sea ?" asked Nelly.

" The ship never was heard from. They supposed she was run down in the night out in the

South Seas somewhere. It was a good while before they gave up expecting news ; but none ever come. I think she set everything by him, and took it very hard losing of him. But there! she 'd never say a word. You 're the freest-spoken Dane I ever saw; but you may take it from your mother's folks. I expect he gave her that whale's tooth with the ship drawn on it that's on the mantelpiece in her room. She may have a sight of other keepsakes, for all I know; but it ain't likely." And here there was a pause, in which Nelly grew sorrowful as she thought of the long waiting for tidings of the missing ship, and of her cousin's solitary life. It was very odd to think of prim Miss Horatia 's being in love with a sailor. There was a young lieutenant in the navy whom Nelly herself liked dearly, and he had gone away on a long voyage. " Perhaps she 's been just as off," said Melissa. " She's dreadful set,

cousin H'ratia is, and sailors is high-tempered men. I 've heard it hinted that he was a fast fellow; and if a woman 's got a good home like this, and's able to do for herself, she'd better stay there. I ain't going to give up a certainty for an uncertainty,— that's what always tell 'em," added Melissa, with great decision, as if she were besieged by lovers; but Nelly smiled inwardly as she thought of the courage it would take to support any one who wished to offer her companion his heart and hand. It would need desperate energy to scale the walls of that garrison.

The green peas were all shelled presently, and Melissa said gravely that she should have to be lazy now until it was time to put in the meat. She was n't used to being helped, unless there was extra work, and she calculated to have one piece of work join on to another. However, it was no account, and she was obliged for the company; and Nelly laughed merrily as she stood washing her hands in the shining old copper basin at the sink. The sun would not be round that side of the house for a long time yet, and the pink and blue morning-glories were still in their full bloom and freshness. They

grew over the window, twined on strings exactly the same distance apart. There was a box crowded full of green houseleeks down at the side of the door; they were straying over the edge, and Melissa stooped stiffly down with an air of disapproval at their untidiness. " They straggle all over everything," said she, " and they 're no kind of use, only Miss's mother, she set everything by 'em. She fetched 'em from home with her when she was married, her mother kep' a box, and they came from England. Folks used to say they was good for bee stings." Then she went into the inner kitchen, and Nelly went slowly away along the flag-stones to the garden from whence she had come. The garden-gate opened with a tired creak, and shut with a clack ; and she noticed how smooth and shiny the wood was where the touch of so many hands had worn it. There was a great pleasure to this gii-1 in finding yherself among such old and well-worn things. She had been for a long time in cities, or at the West; and among the old fashions and ancient possessions of Longfield it seemed to her that everything had its story, and she liked the quietness and unchangeableness with which life seemed to go on from year

to year. She had seen many a dainty or gorgeous garden, but never one that she had liked so well as this, with its herb-bed and its broken rows of currant-bushes, its tall stalks of white lilies, and its wandering rosebushes and honeysuckles, that had bloomed beside the straight paths for so many more summers than she herself had lived. She picked a little bouquet of late red roses, and carried it into the house to put on the parlor table. The wide hall-door was standing open, with its green outer blinds closed, and the old hall was dim and cool. Miss Hora-tia did not like a glare of sunlight, and she abhorred flies with her whole heart. Nelly could hardly see her way through the rooms, it had been so bright out of doors; but she brought the tall champagne-glass of water from the dining-room and put the flowers in their place. Then she looked at two silhouettes which stood on the mantel in carved ebony frames. They were portraits of an uncle of

Miss Dane and his wife. Miss Dane had thought Nelly looked like this uncle the evening before. She could not see the likeness herself; but the pictures suggested something else, and she turned suddenly, and went hurrying up the stairs

to Miss Horatia's own room, where she remembered to have seen a group of silhouettes fastened to the wall. There were seven or eight, and she looked at the young men among them most carefully; but they were all marked with the name of Dane : they were Miss Horatia's uncles and brothers, and our friend hung them on their little brass hooks again with a feeling of disappointment. Perhaps her cousin had a quaint miniature of the lover, painted on ivory, and shut in a worn red morocco case; she hoped she should get a sight of it some day. This /srory of the lost sailor had a wonderful charm for the girl. Miss Horatia had never been so interesting to her before. How she must have mourned for the lover, and missed him, and hoped there would yet be news from the ship! Nelly thought she would tell her own little love-story some day, though there was not much to tell yet, in spite of there being so much to think about. She built a little castle in Spain as she sat in the front window-seat of the upper hall, and dreamed pleasant stories for herself until the sharp noise of the front gate-latch waked her ; and she looked out through the blind to see her cousin coming up the walk.

Miss Horatia looked hot and tired, and her thoughts were not of any fashion of romance. " It is going to be very warm," said she. " I have been worrying ever since I have been gone, because I forgot to ask Andrew to pick those white currants for the minister's wife. I promised that she should have them early this morning. Would you go out to the kitchen and ask Melissa to step in for a moment, my dear ? "

Melissa was picking over red currants to make a pie, and rose from her chair with a little unwillingness. " I guess they could wait until afternoon," said she, as she came back. " Miss H'ratia 's in a fret because she forgot about sending some white currants to the minister's. I told her that Andrew had gone to have the horses shod, and wouldn't be back till near noon. I don't see why part of the folks in the world should kill themselves trying to suit the rest. As long as I have n't got any citron for the cake, I suppose I might go out and pick 'em," added Melissa ungraciously. "I'll get some to set away for tea anyhow."

Miss Dane had a letter to write after she had rested from her walk ; and Nelly soon left her in the dark parlor, and went back

224 A LOST LOVER.

to the sunshiny garden to help Melissa, who seemed to be taking life with more than her usual disapproval. She was sheltered by an enormous gingham sunbonnet.

" I set out to free my mind to your cousin H'ratia this morning," said she, as Nelly crouched down at the opposite side of the bush where she was picking ; " but we can't agree on that p'int, and it's no use. I don't say nothing. You might's well ask the moon to face about and travel the other way as to try to change Miss H'ratia's mind. I ain't going to argue it with her, it ain't my place; I know that as well as anybody. She'd run her feet off for the minister's folks any day ; and though I do say he's a fair preacher, they have n't got a speck o' consideration nor fac'lty; they think the world was made for them, but I think likely they '11 find out it was n't; most folks do. When he first was settled here, I had a fit o' sickness, and he come to see me when I was getting over the worst of it. He did the best he could, I always took it very kind of him; but he made a prayer and he kep' sayin' ' this aged handmaid,' I should think a dozen times. Aged handmaid ! " said Melissa scornfully; " I don't call myself aged

yet, and that was more than ten years ago. I never made pretensions to being younger than I am; but you 'd 'a' thought I was a topplin' eld creatur' going on a hundred."

Nelly laughed. Melissa looked cross, and moved on to the next currant - bush. " So that's why you don't like the minister?" But the question did not seem to please.

" I hope I never should be set against a preacher by such as that." And Nelly hastened to change the subject; but there was to be a last word: " I like to see a minister that's solid minister right straight through, not one of these veneered folks. But old Parson Croden spoilt me for setting under any other preaching."

" I wonder," said Nelly after a little, " if Cousin Horatia has any picture of that Captain Carrick."

" He was n't captain," said Melissa. " I never heard that it was any more than they talked of giving him a ship next voyage."

" And you never saw him ? He never came here to see her ? "

" Bless you, no ! She met with him at Salem, where she was spending the winter, and he went right away to sea. I 've heard a good deal more about it of kte years than

I ever did at the time. I suppose the Salem folks talked about it enough. All I know is, there was other good matches that offered to her since, and could n't get her; and I suppose it was on account of her heart's being buried in the deep with him." And this unexpected bit of sentiment, spoken in Melissa's grum tone, seemed so funny to her young companion, that she bent very low to pick from a currant-twig close to the ground, and could not ask any more questions for some time.

" I have seen her a sight o' times when I knew she was thinking about him," Melissa went on presently, this time with a tenderness in her voice that touched Nelly's heart. " She's been dreadful lonesome. She and the old colonel, her father, was n't much company to each other, and she always kep* everything to herself. The only time she ever said a word to me was one night six or seven years ago this Christmas. They got up a Christmas-tree in the vestry, and she went, and I did too; I guess everybody in the whole church and parish that could crawl turned out to go. The children they inado a dreadful racket. I ? d ha' got my ears took off if I had been so forth-putting when I

was little. I was looking round for Miss H'ratia 'long at the last of the evening, and somebody said they 'd seen her go home. I hurried, and I could n't see any light in the house, and I was afraid she was sick or something. She come and let me in, and I see she had been a-cryin'. I says, ' Have you heard any bad news ?' But she says, No,' and began to cry again, real pitiful. ' I never felt so lonesome in my life,' says she, ' as I did down there. It's a dreadful thing to be left all alone in the world.' I did feel for her; but 1 could n't seem to say a word. I put some pine chips I had handy for morning on the kitchen fire, and I made her up a cup o' good hot tea quick's I could, and took it to her; and I guess she felt better. She never went to bed till three o'clock that night. I could n't shut my eyes till I heard her come upstairs. There! I set everything by Miss H'ratia. I have n't got no folks either. I was left an orphan over to Deerfield, where Miss's mother come from, and she took me out o' the town-farm to bring up. I remember when I come here, I was so small I had a box to stand up on when I helped wash the dishes. There 's nothing I ain't had to make me comfortable,

and I do just as I 'm a mind to, and call in extra help every day of the week if I give the word ; but I 've had my lonesome times, and I guess Miss H'ratia knew."

Nelly was very much touched by this bit of a story, it was a new idea to her that Melissa should have so much affection and be so sympathetic. People never will get over being surprised that chestnut-burrs are not

rough inside as they are outside, and the girl's heart warmed toward the old woman who had spoken with such unlooked-for sentiment and pathos. Melissa went to the house with her basket, and Nelly also went in, but only to put on another hat, and see if it were straight in a minute spent before the old mirror, before she hurried down the long elm-shaded street to buy a pound cf citron for the cake. She left it on the kitchen table when she came back, and nobody ever said anything about it; only there were two delicious pound-cakes — a heart and a round — on a little blue china plate beside Nelly's plate at tea.

After tea, Nelly and Miss Dane sat in the front doorway, — the elder woman in a high-backed chair, and the younger on the door-step. The tree-toads and crickets were tuning up heartily, the stars showed a little through the trees, and the elms looked heavy and black against the sky. The fragrance of the white lilies in the garden blew through the hall. Miss Horatia was tapping the ends of her fingers together. Probably she was not thinking of anything in particular. She had had a very peaceful day, with the exception of the currants; and they had, after all, gone to the parsonage some time before noon. Beside this, the minister had sent word that the delay made no distress; for his wife had unexpectedly gone to Down-ton to pass the day and night. Miss Horatia had received the business letter for which she had been looking for several days; so there was nothing to regret deeply for that day, and there seemed to be nothing for one to dread on the morrow.

" Cousin Horatia," asked Nelly, " are you sure you like having me here? Are you sure I don't trouble you ? "

" Of course not," said Miss Dane, without a bit of sentiment in her tone; " I find it very pleasant having young company, though I am used to being alone ; and I don't mind it as I suppose you would."

" I should mind it very much," said the girl softly.

"You would get used to it, as I have," said Miss Dane. " Yes, dear, I like having you here better and better. I hate to think of your going away." And she smoothed Nelly's hair as if she thought she might have spoken coldly at first, and wished to make up for it. This rare caress was not without its effect.

" I don't miss father and Dick so very much," owned Nelly frankly, "because I have grown used to their coming and going ; but sometimes I miss people — Cousin Horatia, did I ever say anything to you about George Forest ? "

" I think I remember the name," answered Miss Dane.

" He is in the navy, and he has gone a long voyage, and — I think everything of him. I missed him awfully; but it is al-most time to get a letter."

" Does your father approve of him ? " asked Miss Dane, with great propriety. " You are very young yet, and you must not think of such a thing carelessly. I should be so much grieved if you threw away your happiness."

" Oh! we are not really engaged," said Nelly, who felt a little chilled. " I suppose we are, too; only nobody knows yet. Yes, father knows him as well as I do, and he is very fond of him. Of course I should not keep it from father; but he guessed it himself. Only it's such a long cruise, Cousin Horatia, — three years, I suppose, — away off in China and Japan."

" I have known longer voyages than that," said Miss Dane, with a quiver in her voice; and she rose suddenly, and walked away, this grave, reserved woman, who seemed so contented and so comfortable. But when she came back, she asked Nelly a great deal about her lover, and learned more of the girl's life than she ever had before. And they talked together in the pleasantest way about this pleasant subject, which was so close to Nelly's heart, until Melissa brought the candles at ten o'clock, that being the hour of Miss Dane's bedtime.

But that night Miss Dane did not go to bed at ten; she sat by the window in her room, thinking. The moon rose late; and after a little while she blew out her candles, which were burning low. I suppose that the years which had come and gone since the young sailor went away on that last voyage of his had each added to her affection

for him. She was a person who clung the more fondly to youth as she left it the farther behind.

This is such a natural thing; the great sorrows of our youth sometimes become the amusements of our later years ; we can only remember them with a smile. We find that our lives look fairer to us, and we forget what used to trouble us so much, when we look back. Miss Dane certainly had come nearer to truly loving the sailor than she had any one else; and the more she thought of it, the more it became the romance of her life. She no longer asked herself, as she often had done in middle life, whether, if he had lived and had come home, she would have loved and married him. She had minded less and less, year by year, knowing that her friends and neighbors thought her faithful to the love of her youth. Poor, gay, handsome Joe Carrick ! how fond he had been of her, and how he had looked at her that day he sailed away out of Salem Harbor on the brig Chevalier! If she had only known that she never should see him again, poor fellow!

But, as usual, hei- thoughts changed their current a little at the end of her reverie.

Perhaps, after all, loneliness was not so hard to bear as other sorrows. She had had a pleasant life, God had been very good to her, and had spared her many trials, and granted her many blessings. " I am an old woman now," she said to herself. " Things are better as they are ; I can get on by myself better than most women can, and I never should have liked to be interfered with."

Then she shut out the moonlight, and lighted her candles again, with an almost guilty feeling. " What should I say if Nelly sat up till nearly midnight looking out at the moon ? " she thought. " It is very-silly; but this is such a beautiful night. I should like to have her see the moon shining through the tops of the trees." But Nelly was sleeping the sleep of the just and sensible in her own room.

Next morning at breakfast, Nelly was a little conscious of there having been uncommon confidences the night before; but Miss Dane was her usual calm and somewhat formal self, and proposed their making a few calls after dinner, if the weather were not too hot. Nelly at once wondered what she had better wear. There was a certain black

grenadine which Miss Horatia had noticed with approval, and she remembered that the lower ruffle needed hemming, and made up her mind that she would devote most of the time before dinner to that and to some other repairs. So, after breakfast was over, she brought the dress downstairs, with her work-box, and settled herself in the dining-room. Miss Dane usually sat there in the morning; it was a pleasant room, and she could keep an unsuspected watch over the kitchen and Melissa, who did not need watching in the least. I dare say it was for v ythe sake of being within the sound of a voice.

Miss Dane marched in and out that morning ; she went upstairs, and came down again, and was mysteriously busy for a while in the parlor. Nelly was sewing steadily by a window, where one of the blinds was a little way open, and tethered in its place by a string. She hummed a tune to herself over and over: —

; " What will you do, lore, when I am going, With white sails flowing, the seas beyond ?
"

And old Melissa, going to and fro at her work in the kitchen, grumbled out bits of an ancient psalm-tune at intervals. There

seemed to be some connection between these fragments in her mind ; it was like a ledge of rock in a pasture, that sometimes runs under the ground, and then crops out again. Perhaps it was the tune of Windham.

Nelly found that there was a good deal to be done to the grenadine dress when she looked it over critically, and became very diligent. It was quiet in and about the house for a long time, until suddenly she heard the sound of heavy footsteps coming in from the road. The side-door was in a little entry between the room where Nelly sat and the kitchen, and the new-comer knocked loudly. " A tramp," said Nelly to herself; while Melissa came to open the door, wiping her hands hurriedly on her apron.

" I wonder if you could n't give me something to eat," said the man.

" I suppose I could," answered Melissa. " Will you step in ? " Beggars were very few in Longfield, and Miss Dane never wished anybody to go away hungry from her house. It was off the grand highway of tramps; but they were by no means unknown.

Melissa searched among her stores, and

Nelly heard her putting one plate after another on the kitchen table, and thought that the breakfast promised to be a good one, if it were late.

" Don't put yourself out," said the man, as he moved his chair nearer. " I lodged in an old barn three or four miles above here last night, and there did n't seem to be very good board there."

" Going far ? " inquired Melissa concisely.

" Boston," said the man. " I 'm a little too old to travel afoot. Now if I could go by water, it would seem nearer. I 'm more used to the water. This is a royal good piece o' beef. I suppose you could n't put your hand on a mug of cider ? " This was said humbly; but the tone failed to touch Melissa's heart.

" No, I could n't," said she decisively ; so there was an end of that, and the conversation flagged for a time.

Presently Melissa came to speak to Miss Dane, who had just come downstairs. " Could you stay in the kitchen a few minutes ? " she whispered. " There 's an old creatur' there that looks foreign. He came to the door for something to eat, and I gave it to him; but he's miser'ble looking, and I

don't like to leave him alone. I 'm just in the midst o' dressing the chickens. He '11 be through pretty quick, according to the way he 's eating now."

Miss Dane followed her without a word ; and the man half rose, and said, " Good-morning, madam ! " with unusual courtesy. And, when Melissa was out of hearing, he spoke again: " I suppose you have n't any cider ? " to which his hostess answered, " I could n't give you any this morning," in a tone that left no room for argument. He looked as if he had had a great deal too much to drink already.

" How far do you call it from here to Boston ? " he asked, and was told that it was eighty miles.

" I 'm a slow traveler," said he ; " sailors don't take much to walking." Miss Dane asked him if he had been a sailor. " Nothing else," replied the man, who seemed much inclined to talk. He had been eating like a hungry dog, as if he were half-starved, — a slouching, red-faced, untidy-looking old man, with some traces of former good looks still to be discovered in his face. " Nothing else. I ran away to sea when I was a boy, and I followed it until I got so old they would n't ship me even for cook." There was something in his feeling, for once, so comfortable, — perhaps it was being with a lady like Miss Dane, who pitied him, — that lifted his thoughts a little from their usual low level. " It's drink that's been the ruin of me," said he. " I ought to have been somebody. I was nobody's fool when I was young. I got to be mate of a firstrate ship, and there was some talk o' my being captain before long. She was lost that voyage, and three of us were all that was saved ; we got picked up by a Chinese junk. She had the plague aboard of her, and my mates died of it, and I was down myself. It was a hell of a place to be in. When I got ashore I shipped on an old bark that pretended to be coming round the Cape, and she turned out to be a pirate. I just went to the dogs, and I 've gone from bad to worse ever since."

" It's never too late to mend," said Melissa, who came into the kitchen just then for a string to tie the chickens.

" Lord help us, yes, it is! " said the sailor. " It's easy for you to say that. I 'm too old. I ain't been master of this craft for a good while." And he laughed at his melancholy joke.

" Don't say that," said Miss Dane.

"Well, now, what could an old wrack like me do to earn a living ? and who 'd want me if I could? You wouldn't. I don't know when I 've been treated so decent as this before. I 'm all broke down." But his tone was no longer sincere ; he had fallen back on his profession of beggar.

" Could n't you get into some asylum or — there 's the Sailors' Snug Harbor, is n't that for men like you? It seems such a pity for a man of your years to be homeless and a wanderer. Have n't you any friends at all ? " And here, suddenly, Miss Dane's face altered, and she grew very white ; something startled her. She looked as one might who saw a fearful ghost.

" No," said the man ; " but my folks used to be some of the best in Salem. I have n't shown my head there this good while. I was an orphan. My grandmother brought me up. You see, I didn't come back to the States for thirty or forty years. Along at the first of it I used to see men in port that I used to know; but I always dodged 'em, and I was way off in outlandish places. I 've got an awful sight to answer for. I used to have a good wife when I was in Australia.

I don't know where I have n't been, first and last. I was always a gay fellow. I Ve spent as much as a couple o' fortunes, and here I am a-begging. Devil take it! "

Nelly was still sewing in the dining-room ; but, soon after Miss Dane had gone out to the kitchen, one of the doors between had slowly closed itself with a plaintive whine. The round stone which Melissa used to keep it open had been pushed away. Nelly was a little annoyed ; she liked to hear what was going on ; but she was just then holding her work with great care in a place that was hard to sew, so she did not move. She heard the murmur of voices, and thought, after a while, that the old vagabond ought to go away by this time. What could be making her cousin Horatia talk so long with him ? It was not like her at all. He would beg for money, of course, and she hoped Miss Horatia would not give him a single cent.

It was some time before the kitchen-door opened, and the man came out with clumsy, stumbling steps. " I 'm much obliged to you," he said, " and I don't know but it is the last time I '11 get treated as if I was a gentleman. Is there anything I could do

for you round the place ? " he asked hesitatingly, and as if he hoped that his offer would not be accepted.

" No," answered Miss Dane. " No, thank you. Good-by! " and he went away.

The old beggar had been lifted a little above his low life; he fell back again directly before he was out of the gate. " I 'm blessed if she did n't give me a ten-dollar bill! " said he. " She must have thought it was one. I '11 get out o' call as quick as I can; hope she won't find it out, and send anybody after me." Visions of unlimited drinks, and other things in which it was possible to find pleasure, flitted through his stupid mind. " How the old lady stared at me once ! " he thought. " Wonder if she was anybody I used to know ? ' Downton ? ' I don't know as I ever heard of the place." And he scuffed along the dusty road ; and that night he was very drunk, and the next day he went wandering on, God only knows where.

But Nelly and Melissa both heard a strange noise in the kitchen, as if some one had fallen, and they found that Miss Horatia had fainted dead away. It was partly the heat, she said, when she saw their anxious faces as %he came to herself; she had had a little headache all

the morning; it was very hot and close in the kitchen, and the faintness had come upon her suddenly. They helped her to walk into the cool parlor presently, and Melissa brought her a glass of wine, and Nelly sat beside her on a footstool as she lay on the sofa, and fanned her. Once she held her cheek against Miss Horatia's hand for a minute, and she will never know as long as she lives, what a comfort she was that day.

Every one but Miss Dane forgot the old sailor tramp in this excitement that followed his visit. Do you guess already who he was ? But the certainty could not come to you with the chill and horror it did to Miss Dane. There had been something familiar in his look and voice from the first, and

en she had suddenly known him, her lost lover. It was an awful change that the years had made in him. He had truly called himself a wreck; he was like some dreary wreck in its decay and utter ruin, its miserable ugliness and worthlessness, falling to pieces in the slow tides of a lifeless southern sea.

And he had once been her lover, Miss Dane thought bitterly, many times in the days that followed. Not that there was ever

anything asked or promised between them, but they had liked each other dearly, and had parted with deep sorrow. She had thought of him all these years so tenderly; she had believed always that his love had been even greater than her own, and never once had doubted that the missing brig Chevalier had carried with it down into the sea a heart that was true to her.

By little and little this all grew familiar, and she accustomed herself to the knowledge of her new secret. She shuddered at the thought of the misery of a life with him, and she thanked God for sparing her such shame and despair. The distance between them seemed immense. She had always been a person of so much consequence among her friends, and so dutiful and irreproachable a woman. She had not begun to understand what dishonor is in the world ; her life had been shut in by safe and orderly surroundings. It was a strange chance that had brought this wanderer to her door. She remembered his wretched untidiness. She had not liked even to stand near him. She had never imagined him grown old : he had always been young to her. It was a great mercy he had not known her; it would

have been a most miserable position for them both; and yet she thought, with sad surprise, that she had not known she had changed so entirely. She thought of the different ways their roads in life had gone; she pitied him; she cried about him more than once; and she wished that she could know he was dead. He might have been such a brave, good man, with his strong will and resolute courage. God forgive him for the wickedness which his strength had been made to serve! " God forgive him! " said Miss Horatia to herself sadly over and over again. She wondered if she ought to have /let him go away, and so have lost sight of him; but she could not do anything else. She suffered terribly on his account; she had a pity, such as God's pity must be, for even his willful sins.

So her romance was all over with ; yet the townspeople still whispered it to strangers, and even Melissa and Nelly never knew how she had really lost her lover in so strange and sad a way in her latest years. Nobody noticed much change ; but Melissa saw that the whale's tooth disappeared from its place in Miss Ploratia's room, and her old friends said to each other that she began to

show her age a great deal. She seemed really like an old woman now; she was not the woman she had been a year ago.

This is all of the story; but we so often wish, when a story comes to an end, that we knew what became of the people afterward. Shall we believe that Miss Horatia clings more and more fondly to her young cousin Nelly; and that Nelly will stay with her a great deal before she marries, and sometimes afterward, when the lieutenant goes away to sea ? Shall we say that Miss Dane seems as well satisfied and comfortable as ever, though she acknowledges she is not so young as she used to be, and secretly misses something out of her life ? It is the contentment of winter rather than that of summer: the flowers are out of bloom for her now, and under the snow. And Melissa, will not she always be the same, with a quaintness and freshness and toughness like a cedar-tree, to the end of her days ? Let us hope they will live on together and be untroubled this long time yet, the two good women ; and let us wish Nelly much pleasure, and a sweet soberness and fearlessness as she grows older and finds life a harder thing to understand, and a graver thing to know.

THE COURTING OF SISTER WISBY.

ALL the morning there had been an increasing temptation to take an out-door holiday, and early in the afternoon the temptation outgrew my power of resistance. A far-away pasture on the long southwestern slope of a high hill was persistently present to my mind, yet there seemed to be no particular reason why I should think of it. I was not sure that I wanted anything from the pasture, and there was no sign, except the temptation, that the pasture wanted anything of me. But I was on the farther side of as many as three fences before I stopped to think again where I was going, and why.

There is no use in trying to tell another person about that afternoon unless he distinctly remembers weather exactly like it.

o number of details concerning an Arctic ice-blockade will give a single shiver to a child of the tropics. This was one of those

perfect New England days in late summer, when the spirit of autumn takes a first stealthy flight, like a spy, through the ripening country - side, and, with feigned sympathy for those who droop with August heat, puts her cool cloak of bracing air about leaf and flower and human shoulders. Every living thing grows suddenly cheerful and strong ; it is only when you catch sight of a horror-stricken little maple in swampy soil, — a little maple that has second sight and foreknowledge of coming disaster to her race, — only then does a distrust of autumn's friendliness dim your joyful satisfaction.

In midwinter there is always a day when one has the first foretaste of spring; in late August there is a morning when the air is for the first time autumn like. Perhaps it is a hint to the squirrels to get in their first supplies for the winter hoards, or a reminder that summer will soon end, and everybody had better make the most of it. We are always looking forward to the passing and ending of winter, but when summer is here it seems as if summer must always last. As I went across the fields that day, I found myself half lamenting that the world must fade

248 THE COURTING OF SISTER WISBY.

again, even that the best of her budding and bloom was only a preparation for another spring-time, for an awakening beyond the coming winter's sleep.

The sun was slightly veiled ; there was a chattering group of birds, which had gathered for a conference about their early migration. Yet, oddly enough, I heard the voice of a belated bobolink, and presently saw him rise from the grass and hover leisurely, while he sang a brief tune. He was much behind time if he were still a housekeeper ; but as for the other birds, who listened, they cared only for their own notes. An old crow went sagging by, and gave a croak at his despised neighbor, just as a black reviewer croaked at Keats : so hard it is to be just to one's contemporaries. The bobolink was indeed singing out of season, and it was impossible to say whether he really belonged most to this summer or to the next. He might have been delayed on his northward journey ; at any rate, he had a light heart now, to judge from his song, and I wished that I could ask him a few questions, — how he liked being the last man among the bobolinks, and where he had taken singing lessons in the South.

Presently I left the lower fields, and took a path that led higher, where I could look beyond the village to the northern country mountainward. Here the sweet fern grew, thick and fragrant, and I also found myself heedlessly treading on pennyroyal. Near by, in a field corner, I long ago made a most comfortable seat by putting a stray piece of board and bit of rail across the angle of the fences. I have spent many a delightful hour there, in the shade and shelter of a young pitch-pine and a wild-cherry tree, with a lovely outlook toward the village, just far enough away beyond the green slopes and tall elms of the lower meadows. But that day I still had the feeling of being outward bound, and did not turn aside nor linger. The high pasture land grew more and more enticing.

I stopped to pick some blackberries that twinkled at me like beads among their dry vines, and two or three yellow-birds fluttered up from the leaves of a thistle, and then came back again, as if they had complacently discovered that I was only an overgrown yellow-bird, in strange disguise but perfectly harmless. They made me feel as if I were an intruder, though they did not offer to

peck at me, and we parted company very soon. It was good to stand at last on the great shoulder of the hill. The wind was coming in from the sea, there was a fine fragrance from the pines, and the air grew sweeter every moment. I took new pleasure on the thought that in a piece of wild pasture land like this one may get closest to Nature, and subsist upon what she gives of her own free will. There have been no drudging, heavy-shod ploughmen to overturn the soil, and vex it into yielding artificial crops. Here one has to take just what Nature is pleased to give, whether one is a yellow-bird or a human being. It is very good entertainment for a summer wayfarer, and I am asking my reader now to share the winter provision which I harvested that day. Let us hope that the small birds are also faring well after their fashion, but I give them an anxious thought while the snow goes hurrying in long waves across the buried fields, this windy winter night.

I next went farther down the hill, and got a drink of fresh cool water from the brook, and pulled a tender sheaf of sweet flag beside it. The mossy old fence just beyond was the last barrier between me and

the pasture which had sent an invisible messenger earlier in the day, but I saw that somebody else had come first to the rendezvous : there was a brown gingham cape-bonnet and a sprigged shoulder-shawl bobbing up and down, a little way off among the junipers. I had taken such uncommon pleasure in being alone that I instantly felt a sense of disappointment; then a warm glow of pleasant satisfaction rebuked-my selfishness. This could be no one but dear old Mrs. Goodsoe, the friend of my childhood and fond dependence of my maturer years. I had not seen her for many weeks, but here she was, out on one of her famous campaigns for herbs, or perhaps just returning from a blueberrying expedition. I approached with care, so as not to startle the gingham bonnet ; but she heard the rustle of the bushes against my dress, and looked up quickly, as she knelt, bending over the turf. In that position she was hardly taller than the luxuriant junipers themselves.

"I 'm a-gittin' in my mulleins," she said briskly, "an* I 've been thinking o' you these twenty times since I come out o' the house. I begun to believe you must ha' forgot me at last."

"I have been away from home," I explained. " Why don't you get in your pennyroyal too ? There 's a great plantation of it beyond the next fence but one."

" Pennyr'yal! " repeated the dear little old woman, with an air of compassion for inferior knowledge; " 't ain't the right time, darlin'. Pennyr'yal's too rank now. But for mulleins this day is prime. I 've got a dreadful graspin' fit for 'em this year ; seems if I must be goin' to need 'em extry. I feel like the squirrels must when they know a hard winter's comin'." And Mrs. Goodsoe bent over her work again, while I stood by and watched her carefully cut the best full-grown leaves with a clumsy pair of scissors, which might have served through at least half a century of herb-gathering. They were fastened to her apron-strings by a long piece of list.

" I 'm going to take my jack-knife and help you," I suggested, with some fear of refusal. " I just passed a flourishing family of six or seven heads that must have been growing on purpose for you."

"Now be keerful, dear heart," was the anxious response; " choose 'em well. There 's odds in mulleins same's there is in

angels. Take a plant that's all run up to stalk, and there ain't but little goodness in the leaves. This one I 'm at now must ha' been stepped on by some creatur' and blighted of its bloom, and the leaves is han'-some! When I was small I used to have a notion that Adam an' Eve must a took mulleins fer their winter wear. Ain't they just like flannel, for all the world ? I 've had experience, and I know there's plenty of sickness might be saved to folks if they 'd quit horse-radish and such fiery, exasperating things, and use mullein drarves in proper season. Now I shall spread these an' dry 'em nice on my spare floor in the garrit, an' come to steam 'em for use along in the winter there be the vally of the whole summer's goodness in 'em, sartin." And she snipped away with the dull scissors, while I listened respectfully, and took great pains to have my part of the harvest present a good appearance.

" This is most too dry a head," she added presently, a little out of breath. " There I I can tell you there's win'rows o' young doctors, bilin' over with book-larnin', that is truly ignorant of what to do for the sick, or how to p'int out those paths that well

people foller toward sickness. Book-fools I call 'em, them young men, an' some on 'em never '11 live to know much better, if they git to be Methuselahs. In my time eVery middle-aged woman, who had brought up a family, had some proper ideas o' dealin' with complaints. I won't say but there was some fools amongst them, but I 'd rather take my chances, unless they 'd forsook herbs and gone to dealin' with patent stuff. Now my mother really did sense the use of herbs and roots. I never see anybody that come up to her. She was a meek-looking woman, but very understanding mother was."

" Then that's where you learned so much yourself, Mrs. Goodsoe," I ventured to say.

" Bless your heart, I don't hold a candle to her; 't is but little I can recall of what she used to say. No, her 1'arnin' died with her," said my friend, in a self-depreciating tone. " Why, there was as many as twenty kinds of roots alone that she used to keep by her, that I forget the use of; an' I 'm sure I should n't know where to find the most of 'em, any. There was an herb " — airb, she called it — " an herb called master-wort, that she used to get way from Penn-sylvany; and she used to think everything

of noble-liverwort, but I never could seem to get the right effects from it as she could.

Though I don't know as she ever really did use master wort where somethin' else would n't a served. She had a cousin married out in Pennsylvany that used to take pains to get it to her every year or two, and so she felt 't was important to have it. Some set more by such things as come from a distance, but I rec'lect mother always used to maintain that folks was meant to be doctored with the stuff that grew right about 'em; 't was sufficient, an' so ordered. That was before the whole population took to livin' on wheels, the way they do now. 'T was never my idee that we was meant to know what's goin' on all over the world to once. There 's goin' to be some sort of a set-back one o' these days, with these telegraphs an' things, an' letters comin' every hand's turn, and folks leavin' their proper work to answer 'em. I may not live to see it. 'T was allowed to be difficult for folks to git about in old times, or to git word across the country, and they stood in their lot an' place, and weren't all just alike, either, same as pine-spills."

We were kneeling side by side now, as if

in penitence for the march of progress, hut we laughed as we turned to look at each other.

" Do you think it did much good when everybody brewed a cracked quart mug of herb-tea?" I asked, walking away on my knees to a new mullein.

" I 've always lifted my voice against the practice, far 's I could," declared Mrs. Good-soe ; " an' I won't deal out none o' the herbs I save for no such nonsense. There was three houses along our road, — I call no names, — where you couldn't go into the livin' room without findin' a mess o' herb-tea drorin' on the stove or side o' the fireplace, winter or summer, sick or well. One was thoroughwut, one would be camomile, and the other, like as not, yellow dock ; but they all used to put in a little new rum to git out the goodness, or keep it from spilin'." (Mrs. Goodsoe favored me with a knowing smile.) " Land, how mother used to laugh! But, poor creaturs, they had to work hard, and I guess it never done 'em a mite o' harm ; they was all good herbs. I wish you could hear the quawkin' there used to be when they was indulged with a real case o' sickness. Everybody would collect from

far an' near ; you 'd see 'em coming along the road and across the pastures then ; everybody clainorin' that nothin' would n't do no kind o' good but her choice o ? teas or drarves to the feet. I wonder there was a babe lived to grow up in the whole lower part o' the town ; an' if nothin' else 'peared to ail 'em, word was passed about that't was likely Mis' So-and-So's last young one was goin' to be foolish. Land, how they 'd gather! I know one day the doctor come to Widder Peck's and the house was crammed so 't he could scercely git inside the door; and he says, just as polite, ' Do send for some of the neighbors ! ' as if there wa'n't a soul to turn to, right or left. You 'd ought to seen 'em begin to scatter."

" But don't you think the cars and telegraphs have given people more to interest them, Mrs. Goodsoe ? Don't you believe people's lives were narrower then, and more taken up with little things ? " I asked, unwisely, being a product of modern times.

" Not one mite, dear," said my companion stoutly. " There was as big thoughts then as there is now; these times was born o' them. The difference is in folks themselves ; but now, instead o' doin' their own house-

keepin' and watchin' their own 'neighbors, — though that was carried to excess, — they git word that a niece's child is ailin' the other side o' Massachusetts, and they drop everything and git on their best clothes, and off they jiggit in the cars. 'Tis a bad sign when folks wears out their best clothes faster 'n they do their every-day ones. The other side o' Massachusetts has got to look after itself by rights. An' besides that, Sunday-keepin' 's all gone out o' fashion. Some lays it to one thing an' some another, but some o' them old ministers that folks are all a-sighin' for did preach a lot o' stuff that wa'n't nothin' but chaff; 't wa'n't the word o' God out o'either Old Testament or New. But everybody went to meetin' and heard it, and come home, and was set to fightin' with their next door neighbor over it. Now I 'm a believer, and I try to live a Christian life, but I 'd as soon hear a surveyor's book read out, figgers an' all, as try to get any simple truth out o' most sermons. It's them as is most to blame."

"What was the matter that day at Widow Peck's?" I hastened to ask, for I knew by experience that the good, clear-minded soul beside me was apt to grow unduly vexed and distressed when she contemplated the state of religious teaching.

"Why, there wa'n't nothin' the matter, only a gal o' Miss Peck's had met with a dis'pintment and had gone into screechin' fits. 'T was a rovin' creatur' that had come along hayin' time, and he'd gone off an' forsook her betwixt two days; nobody ever knew what become of him. Them Pecks was * Good Lord, anybody! ' kind o' gals, and took up with whoever they could get. One of 'em married Heron, the Irishman; they lived in that little house that was burnt this summer, over on the edge o' the plains. He was a good-hearted creatur', with a laughin' eye and a clever word for everybody. He was the first Irishman that ever came this way, and we was all for gettin' a look at him, when he first used to go by. Mother's folks was what they call Scotch-Irish, though; there was an old race of 'em settled about here. They could foretell events, some on 'em, and had the second sight. I know folks used to say mother's grandmother had them gifts, but mother was never free to speak about it to us. She remembered her well, too."

" I suppose that you mean old Jim Heron, who was such a famous fiddler ? " I asked
260 THE COURTING OF SISTER WISBY.
with great interest, for I am always delighted to know more about that rustic hero, parochial Orpheus that he must have been !

" Now, dear heart, I suppose you don't remember him, do you ? " replied Mrs. Goodsoe, earnestly. " Fiddle ! He 'd about break your heart with them tunes of his, or else set your heels flying up the floor in a jig, though you was minister o' the First Parish and all wound up for a funeral prayer. I tell ye there ain't no tunes sounds like them used to. It used to seem to me summer nights when I was comin' along the plains road, and he set by the window playin', as if there was a bewitched human creatur' in that old red fiddle o' his. He could make it sound just like a woman's voice tellin' somethin' over and over, as if folks could help her out o' her sorrows if she could only make 'em understand. I 've set by the stone-wall and cried as if my heart was broke, and dear knows it wa'n't in them days. How he would twirl off them jigs and dance tunes! He used to make somethin' han'some out of 'em in fall an' winter, playin' at huskins and dancin' parties; but he was nnstidcly by spells, as he got along in years, and never knew what it was to be forehanded. Everybody felt bad when he died; you could n't help likin' the creatur'. He 'd got the gift — that's all you could say about it.

"There was a Mis' Jerry Foss, that lived over by the brook bridge, on the plains road, that had lost her husband early, and was left with three child'n. She set the world by 'em, and was a real pleasant, ambitious little woman, and was workin' on as best she could with that little farm, when there come a rage o' scarlet fever, and her boy and two girls was swept off and laid dead within the same week. Every one o' the neighbors did what they could, but she 'd had no sleep since they was taken sick, and after the funeral she set there just like a piece o' marble, and would only shake her head when you spoke to her. They all thought her reason would go ; and 't would certain, if she could n't have shed tears. An' one o' the neighbors — 't was like mother's sense, but it might have been somebody else —spoke o' Jim Heron. Mother an' one or two o' the women that knew her best was in the house with her. 'T was right in the edge o' the woods and some of us younger ones was over by the wall on the other side of the road where there v/as a couple of old willows, — I remember just

how the brook clamp felt; and we kept quiet's we could, and some other folks come along down the road, and stood waitin' on the little bridge, hopin' somebody'd come out, I suppose, and they 'd git news. Everybody was wrought up, and felt a good deal for her, you know. By an' by Jim Heron come stealin' right out o' the shadows an' set down on the doorstep, an' 't was a good while before we heard a sound ; then, oh, dear me! 't was what the whole neighborhood felt for that mother all spoke in the notes, an' they told me afterwards that Mis' Foss's face changed in a minute, and she come right over an' got into my mother's lap, — she was a little woman, — an' laid her head down, and there she cried herself into a blessed sleep. After awhile one o' the other women stole out an' told the folks, and we all went home. He only played that one tune.

" But there!" resumed Mrs. Goodsoe, after a silence, during which my eyes were filled with tears. " His wife always complained that the fiddle made her nervous. She never 'peared to think nothin' o' poor Heron after she 'd once got him."

" That's often the way," said I, with harsh cynicism, though I had no guilty person in my mind at the moment; and we went straying off, not very far apart, up through the pasture. Mrs. Goodsoe cautioned me that we must not get so far off that we could not get back the same day. The sunshine began to feel very hot on our backs, and we both turned toward the shade. We had already collected a large bundle of mullein leaves, which were carefully laid into a clean, calico apron, held together by the four corners, and proudly carried by me, though my companion regarded them with anxious eyes. We sat down together at the edge of the pine woods, and Mrs. Goodsoe proceeded to fan herself with her limp cape-bonnet.

" I declare, how hot it is ! The east wind's all gone again," she said. " It felt so cool this forenoon that I overburdened myself with as thick a petticoat as any I 've got. I 'm despri't afeared of having a chill, now that I ain't so young as once. I hate to be housed up."

" It's only August, after all," I assured her unnecessarily, confirming my statement by taking two peaches out of my pocket, and laying them side by side on the brown pine needles between us.

" Dear sakes alive! " exclaimed the old

264 THE COURTING OF SISTER W1SDY.

lady, with evident pleasure. " Where did you get them, now? Does n't anything t;i>te twice better out-o'-doors ? I ain't had such a peach for years. Do le's keep the stones, an' I '11 plant 'em ; it only takes four year for a peach pit to come to bearing, an' I guess I 'm good for four year, 'thout I meet with some accident."

I could not help agreeing, or taking a fond look at the thin little figure, and her wrinkled brown face and kind, twinkling eyes. She looked as if she had properly dried herself, by mistake, with some of her mullein leaves, and was likely to keep her goodness, and to last the longer in consequence. There never was a truer, simple-hearted soul made out of the old-fashioned country dust than Mrs. Goodsoe. I thought, as I looked away from her across the wide country, that nobody was left in any of the farm-houses so original, so full of rural wisdom and reminiscence, so really able and dependable, as she. And nobody had made better use of her time in a world foolish enough to sometimes undervalue medicinal herbs.

When we had eaten our peaches we still sat under the pines, and I was not without pride when I had poked about in the ground with a little twig, and displayed to my crony a long fine root, bright yellow to the eye, and a wholesome bitter to the taste.

"Yis, dear, goldthread," she assented indulgently. " Seems to me there's more of it than anything except grass an' hardhack. Good for canker, but no better than two or three other things I can call to mind; but I always lay in a good wisp of it, for old times' sake. Now, I want to know why you should a bit it, and took away all the taste o' your nice peach ? I was just thinkin' what a han'sorae entertainment we 've had. I 've got so I 'sociate certain things with certain folks, and goldthread was sornethin' Lizy Wisby couldn't keep house without, no ways whatever. I believe she took so much it kind o' puckered her disposition."

" Lizy Wisby ? " I repeated inquiringly.

" You knew her, if ever, by the name of Mis' Deacon Brimblecom," answered my friend, as if this were only a brief preface to further information, sj I waited with respectful expectation. Mrs. Goodsoe had grown tired out in the sun, and a good story would be an excuse for sufficient rest. It was a most lovely place where we sat, halfway up the long hillside; for my part, I was perfectly contented and happy. " You 've often heard of Deacon Brimblecom ? " she asked, as if a great deal depended upon his being properly introduced.

" I remember him," said I. " They called him Deacon Brimfull, you know, and he used to go about with a witch-ha/cl branch to show people where to dig wells."

" That's the one," said Mrs. Goodsoe, laughing. " I did n't know's you could go so far back. I 'm always divided between whether you can remember everything I can, or are only a babe in arms."

" I have a dim recollection of there being something strange about their marriage," I suggested, after a pause, which began to appear dangerous. I was so much afraid the subject would be changed.

" I can tell you all about it," I was quickly answered. " Deacon Brimblecora was very pious accordin' to his lights in his early years. He lived way back in the country then, and there come a rovin' preacher along, and set everybody up that way all by the ears. I 've heard the old folks talk it over, but I forget most of his doctrine, except some of his followers was persuaded they could dwell among the an-

gels while yet on airth, and this Deacon Brimfull, as you call him, felt sure he was called by the voice of a spirit bride. So he left a good, deservin' wife he had, an' four children, and built him a new house over to the other side of the land he 'd had from his father. They didn't take much pains with the buildin', because they expected to be translated before long, and then the spirit brides and them folks was goin' to appear and divide up the airth amongst 'em, and the world's folks and on-believers was goin' to serve 'em or be sent to torments. They had meetins about in the school-houses, an' all sorts o' goins on ; some on 'em went crazy, but the deacon held on to what wits he had, an' by an' by the spirit bride did n't turn out to be much of a housekeeper, an' he had always been used to good livin', so he sneaked home ag'in. One o' mother's sisters married up to Ash Hill, where it all took place ; that's how I come to have the particulars."

" Then how did he come to find his Eliza Wisby?" I inquired. "Do tell me the whole story; you've got mullein leaves enough."

" There's all yisterday's at home, if I haven't," replied Mrs. Goodsoe. "The way he come a-courtin' o' Sister Wisby was this: she went a-courtin' o' him.

" There was a spell he lived to home, and then his poor wife died, and he had a spirit bride in good earnest, an' the child'n was placed about with his folks and hers, for they was both out o' good families ; and I don't know what come over him, but he had another pious fit that looked for all the world like the real thing. He had n't no family cares, and he lived with his brother's folks, and turned his land in with theirs. He used to travel to every meetin' an' conference that was within reach of his old sorrel hoss's feeble legs; he j'ined the Christian Baptists that was just in their early prime, and he was a great exhorter, and got to be called deacon, though I guess he wa'n't deacon, 'less it was for a spare hand when deacon timber was scercer'n usual. An' one time there was a four days' protracted ^eetin' to the church in the lower part of 7 the town. 'T was a real solemn time ; something more'n usual was goin' forward, an' they collected from the whole country round. Women folks liked it, an' the men too; it give 'em a change, an' they was quartered

round free, same as conference folks now. Some on 'em, for a joke, sent Silas Brimblecom up to Lizy Wisby's, though she 'd give out she could n't accommodate nobody, because of expectin' her cousin's folks. Everybody knew 't was a lie; she was amazin' close considerin' she had plenty to do with. There was a streak that wa'n't just right somewheres in Lizy's wits, I always thought. She was very kind in case o' sickness, I '11 say that for her.

" You know where the house is, over there on what they call Windy Hill ? There the deacon went, all unsuspectin', and 'stead o' Lizy 's resentin' of him she put in her own hoss, and they come back together to evenin' meetin'. She was prominent among the sect herself, an' he bawled and talked, and she bawled and talked, an' took up more 'n the time allotted in the exercises, just as if they was showin' off to each other what they was able to do at expoundin'. Everybody was laughin' at 'em after the meetin' broke up, and that next day an' the next, an' all through, they was constant, and seemed to be havin' a beautiful occasion. Lizy had always give out she scorned the men, but when she got a chance at a particular one

270 THE COURTING OF SISTKR W1SBY.

't was altogether different, and the deacon seemed to please her somehow or 'nother, and — There! you don't want to listen to this old stuff that's past an' gone ? "

" Oh yes, I do," said I.

" I run on like a clock that's onset her striking hand," said Mrs. Goodsoe mildly. " Sometimes my kitchen timepiece goes on half the forenoon, and I says to myself the day before yisterday I would let it be a warnin', and keep it in mind for a check on my own speech. The next news that was heard was that the deacon an' Lizy — well, opinions differed which of 'em had spoke first, but them fools settled it liefore the protracted meetiu' was over, and give away their hearts before he started for home. They considered 't would be wise, though, considerin' their short acquaintance, to take one another on trial a spell; 't was Lizy's notion, and she asked him why he would n't come over and stop with her till spring, and then, if they both continued to like, they could git married any time 't was convenient. Lizy, she come and talked it over with mother, and mother disliked to offend her, but she spoke pretty plain ; and Lizy felt hurt, an' thought they was showin' excellent

judgment, so much harm come from hasty unions and folks comin' to a realizin' sense of each other's failin's when 't was too late.

" So one day our folks saw Deacon Brim-full a-ridin' by with a gre't coopful of hens in the back o' his wagon, and bundles o' stuff tied on top and hitched to the exes underneath ; and he riz a hymn just as he passed the house, and was speedin' the old sorrel with a wilier switch. 'T was most Thanksgivin' time, an' sooner 'n she expected him. New Year's was the time she set; but he thought he 'd better come while the roads was fit for wheels. They was out to meetin' together Thanksgivin' Day, an' that used to be a gre't season for marryin' ; so the young folks nudged each other, and some on' 'em ventured to speak to the couple as they come down the aisle. Lizy carried it off real well; she wa'n't afraid o' what nobody said or thought, and so home they went. They 'd got out her yaller sleigh and her hoss ; she never would ride after the deacon's poor old creatur', and I believe it died long o' the winter from stiffenin' up.

"Yes," said Mrs. Goodsoe emphatically, after we had silently considered the situation for a short space of time, — " yes, there

was consider'ble talk, now I tell you ! The raskil boys pestered 'em just about to death for a while. They used to collect up there an' rap on the winders, and they 'd turn out all the deacon's hens 'long at nine o'clock 'o night, and chase 'em all over the dingle; an' one night they even lugged the pig right out o' the sty, and shoved it into the back entry, an' run for their lives. They 'd stuffed its mouth full o' somethin', so it could n't squeal till it got there. There wa'n't a sign o' nobody to be seen when Lizy hasti-d out with the light, and she an' the deacon had to persuade the creatur' back as best they could ; 't was a cold night, and they said it took 'em till towards mornin'. You see the deacon was just the kind of a man that a hog would n't budge for ; it takes a masterful man to deal with a hog. Well, there was no end to the works nor the talk, but Lizy left 'em pretty much alone. She did 'pear kind of dignified about it, I must say!"

"And then, were they married in the spring?"

" I was tryin' to remember whether it was just before Fast Day or just after," responded my friend, with a careful look at

the sun, which was nearer the west than either of us had noticed. " I think likely 't was along in the last o' April, any way some of us looked out o' the window one Monday mornin' early, and says, * For goodness' sake! Lizy 's sent the deacon home again !' His old sorrel havin' passed away, he was ridin' in Ezry Welsh's hoss-cart, with his hen-coop and more bundles than he had when he come, and he looked as meechin' as ever you see. Ezry was drivin', and he let a glance fly swiftly round to see if any of us was lookin' out; an' then I declare if he did n't have the malice to turn right in towards the barn, where he see my oldest brother, Joshuay, an' says he real natural, ' Joshuay, just step out with your wrench. I believe I hear my kingbolt rat-tlin' kind o' loose.' Brother, he went out an' took in the sitooation, an' the deacon bowed kind of stiff. Joshuay was so full o' laugh, and Ezry Welsh, that they could n't look one another in the face. There wa'n't nothing ailed the kingbolt, you know, an' when Josh riz up he says, * Goin' up country for a spell, Mr. Brimblecom ?'

" ' I be,' says the deacon, lookin' dreadful mortified and cast down.

"' Ain't things turned out well with you an' Sister Wisby?' says Joshuay. 'You had ought to remember that the woman is the weaker vessel.' •

"'Hang her, let her carry less sail, the deacon bu'st out, and he stood right up an' shook his fist there by the hencoop, he was so mad; an' Ezry's hoss was a young creatur', an' started up an set the deacon right over backwards into the chips. We did n't know but he 'd broke his neck ; but when he see the women folks runniu' out, he jumped up quick as a cat, an' clim' into the cart, an' off they went. Ezry said he told him that he could n't git along /with Lizy, she was so fractious in thundery weather ; if there was a rumble in the daytime she must go right to bed an' screech, and if 't was night she must git right up an' go an' call him out of a sound sleep. But everybody knew he 'd never a gone home unless she 'd sent him.

" Somehow they made it up agin right away, him an' Lizy, and she had him back. She 'd been countin' all along on not havin' to hire nobody to work about the gardin an' so on, an' she said she wa'n't goin' to let him have a whole winter's board for nothin'. So

the old hens was moved back, and they was married right off fair an' square, an' I don't know but they got along well as most folks. He brought his' youngest girl down to live with 'em after a while, an' she was a real treasure to Lizy; everybody spoke well o r Phebe Brimblecom. The deacon got over his pious fit, and there was consider'ble work in him if you kept right after him. He was an ainazin' cider-drinker, and he airnt the name you know him by in his latter days. Lizy never trusted him with nothin', but she kep' him well. She left everything she owned to Phebe, when she died, 'cept somethin' to satisfy the law. There, they 're all gone now : seems to me sometimes, when I get thinkin,' as if I 'd lived a thousand years! "

I laughed, but I found that Mrs. Good-soe's thoughts had taken a serious turn.

" There, I come by some old graves down here in the lower edge of the pasture," she said as we rose to go. " I could n't help thinking how I should like to be laid right out in the pasture ground, when my time comes; it looked sort o' comfortable, and I have ranged these slopes so many summers. Seems as if I could see right up through the

turf and tell when the rnther was pleasant, and get the goodness o' the sweet fern. Mow, dear, just hand me my apernful o' mulleins out o' the shade. I hope you won't come to need none this winter, but I '11 dry some special for you."

"I 'm going home by the road," said I, " or else by the path across the meadows, so I will walk as far as the house with you. Are n't you pleased with my company ?" for she demurred at my going the least bit out of the way.

So we strolled toward the little gray house, with our plunder of mullein leaves slung on a stick which we carried between us. Of course I went in to make a call, as if I had not seen my hostess before ; she is the last maker of muster-gingerbread, and before I came away I was kindly measured for a pair of mittens.

" You be sure to come an' see them two peach-trees after I get 'em well growin'?" Mrs. Goodsoe called after me when I had said good-by, and was almost out of hearing down the road.

THE END

Made in the USA
Columbia, SC
03 January 2020